For Elizabeth

Gravitation cannot be held
responsible for people falling in love.

—Albert Einstein

I never fall apart,
because I never fall together.

—Andy Warhol

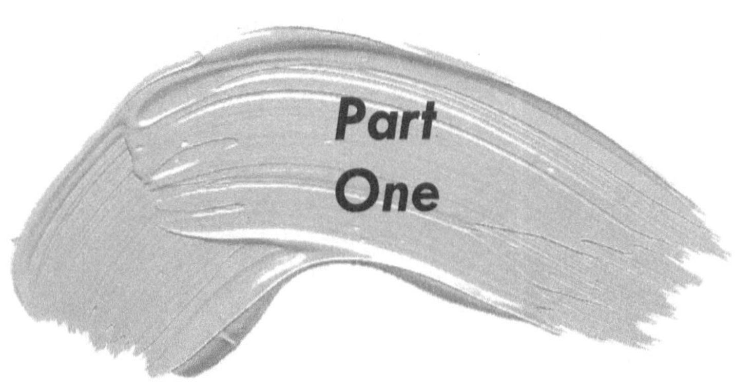
Part
One

Chapter 1

THE WALL THAT separated us began to vibrate with a familiar 60-hertz hum, and I knew what was coming next: a sound akin to automatic weapon fire, round after round, interspersed with terrifyingly high-pitched harmonic squeals. After that came a power chord progression followed by several minor arpeggios, the same pattern repeatedly. Harry—better known by his ridiculous stage name, Pigeonhole—paused for a moment to let his guitar pickups feedback through the amplifier. I checked my phone. 5:44 a.m. For Pigeonhole, this time of morning was often the end of a long night out playing guitar at some hellhole suburban rock club and then drinking himself to sleep, but not before waking up half the building with one of his sloppy, intoxicated, and totally unnecessary soundchecks. I thought of Pigeonhole as not much more than a clown, a caricature of a failed musician, or at best a foil to my own artistic ambitions. I admit he made that a rather easy conclusion to draw.

Sara lay next to me, her arm curled up over her head, her armpit countersunk in shadow, her straight black hair spread across the pillowcase. True to form, she was still asleep. Sara could always sleep, in noise or silence, in heat or cold, in dark or light. It didn't matter. She could sleep outside in the sun, in a moving car, in an airplane rocked by turbulence, or on a drafty wooden floor. To her, sleep was a game. For me, sleep was a test of will for so many reasons— and one of them was living next door to Pigeonhole.

To call Sara my girlfriend was insufficient. She moved through my life like a weather system, wielding power over me at all times. But the elemental power she held when she slept was like nothing else—no drug, no drink, no promise from the gods could have eclipsed it. She knew that I occasionally lay awake for hours staring at her, absorbing her darkling beauty, wondering what she saw in me. Whatever it was, it was more than I saw in myself. In fact, the only thing I saw in myself was a depressed and failing artist whose dead mother haunted him day and night. Whether she was an apparition or a hallucination didn't really matter. What mattered was the fact that she was ever there at all.

Having absorbed as much of Sara's sweetness as I could in that moment, I reached over and touched her hair, then her cheek, tracing a line along her jawbone. She pulled the blanket, rolled over, and pressed her face into the pillow.

"William, you've got to stop using that turpentine," she said in a muffled voice. "This place stinks."

"Are you kidding me?" My voice was still a little raspy. "I love the smell of turpentine in the morning."

Sara groaned into her pillow. "At least open the window for a minute. The smell builds up overnight. It can't be good to breathe this stuff."

She was right. I needed to go back to the odorless paint thinner. But I believed the smell of turpentine was something that attracted my mother, whose presence—for better or worse—was necessary if I was going to finish the paintings I needed for my first solo exhibition.

I got up from the bed, cracked open the window, and put on the same pair of jeans and gray turtleneck I had worn the previous two days. It was early spring in Minneapolis, and my drafty, poorly heated apartment was bone-chillingly cold in the mornings. With the window open, we might as well have been camping. I shivered as I opened the door to the hallway where Pigeonhole's squealing guitar reverberated even more loudly. A hand-painted gold star bearing his stage name in all caps, PIGEONHOLE, hung from his door. I knocked on the star as he launched into a rendition of Van Halen's "Eruption." Glitter fell from the star, dusting my toes. Even if he had heard me, he had no intention of stopping.

I gave up and walked down the hall to the bathroom we shared. The St. Jude was the last of the old Minneapolis tenement buildings that maintained the old-world tradition of shared bathrooms between apartments. It was an awful arrangement, but my apartment was far cheaper and far more spacious than any other building in town—a 1,500-square-foot studio for under $700 a month, a throwback to the 1990s, not unlike Pigeonhole himself.

In the bathroom, a half-dozen of Pigeonhole's filthy towels were piled in the corner. By way of Post-it notes, I had made him aware many times of the coin-operated washing machines in the building's basement. These notes were ignored, just as my knocking was. "I love that I can ignore you so well," he once said. "It's like my superpower. That, and the Phrygian dominant scale." I imagined he was simply holding out hope (just as he maintained hope for that long-elusive record deal) that one day his girlfriend, Tanya, would finally give in and do a few loads of laundry for him. No such luck. I was scared to imagine what might be alive—mushrooms? algae? squirrels?—beneath those towels.

I twisted the faucet and waited for the water to run warm. This took nearly a minute. As I rinsed my face and brushed my teeth, I saw that Pigeonhole had dropped a piece of bread smeared with strawberry jam, jam side down, on the floor next to the bathtub. The open jar of jam sat on the edge of the tub with a knife protruding. Not a butter knife; a bowie knife. I rinsed the blade and slid it into the medicine cabinet, then closed the jar and tossed the bread into the toilet. I poured Listerine on the floor to discourage the cockroaches.

Back in my apartment, Sara was up and pouring a cup of cold coffee from the day before. She looked to be in a hurry.

"That coffee's from yesterday," I said. "And it's hazelnut. You hate that."

"It's fine," she said. "I have to be at work in less than an hour, and I'm exhausted." She worked part time at a diner downtown, though she didn't really need the money, considering her generous father's high income as a preeminent reconstructive surgeon.

I put a kettle on the stove anyway, as I had a long day of painting ahead of me. Sara made her way down the hallway to the bathroom.

It had been just over a year since I first met Sara. In that year, my life had been taken over with the force of a coup d'etat. Sara was feisty, compact, and intense. Her dark hair stood in stark contrast to her waxy, pale complexion. Her head, round and nimble as a blackbird's, seemed scarcely attached to her slender neck, as if it might take flight at the slightest provocation. Her irises, almost as dark as her pupils if not for a few gold-green flecks, lent her gaze an ancient, stonelike quality. The way she swung her hips, the way she shook her hair, the way she wiggled her feet into her shoes—I found it all utterly spellbinding. Put another way, I was screwed.

When Sara returned from the bathroom, I had positioned myself in front of my easel and was staring at the painting I had begun the night before. Just as I was about to suggest to Sara that she come back later that night to assess my progress, my mother suddenly appeared, phasing out of the wall in her ever-present white dress, long and flowing, covered in ash. Her hair was braided with dead flowers, and her face, though caked in soot, could have been my own—the same narrow nose, the same oval face and tall forehead, the same eyebrows like two wiper blades at the ready. She held a squint suggesting that the entire world were a mild irritant. It was like looking in a mirror.

As always—thank God—Sara couldn't see her, and these appearances hardly startled me anymore, at least not outwardly. Then again, was I actually seeing anything beyond a figment of my own imagination? I edged back from the easel, trying to give my mother some space while making a show of appraising the canvas, as if the next brushstroke required a deep and deliberate calculation on my part. Sara gulped the rest of her coffee in silence. My mother ignored the two of us and moved toward the easel, shaking her head in apparent disappointment with my lack of progress. If Sara hadn't been there, my mother might have seized a brush and set about revising everything I had attempted, as was her habit, elevating the work to her higher level of artistic standards. But instead, she turned away and drifted past me toward the window. Something on the street caught her interest, and the next moment she melted through the closed window and was gone.

"What are you looking at?"

"Just checking the light. Gotta work on this painting all day, and I might move it closer to the window since it's cloudy."

"You're zoned in on painting even before I walk out the door?" Sara, of course, had no idea what I had just seen, and I wasn't about to tell her. The look on her face told me that nothing I could have said might have helped. Especially not the truth.

"I thought I had an idea of what I'd work on next. I didn't want to lose my train of thought."

"I think what you should work on next is grinding some beans. You're right, this hazelnut sucks."

Sara started dressing while I plugged in my coffee grinder. By this point, Pigeonhole had stopped playing, and the building was quiet for the moment. I didn't want to spoil it with the cacophony of the grinder, so I dug around in the cupboard for an old bag of ground dark roast.

She wrapped herself in her black wool coat, the one that had belonged to her mother, who, it turned out, had died the same year as my mother when we were both ten, but who had, at least for all anyone knew, never returned. The coat was a charming advertisement for a certain type of affluence. The kind that could be forgiven. The source of said affluence was not only Sara's father. Her mother had also been a physician, specifically a psychiatrist, and she had dressed like one. The coat was a little small on Sara, adding another layer of charm, and therefore could even more easily be forgiven.

Sara stuffed her hands into the coat pockets. She pulled out two red gloves.

"Jeez, I've been looking everywhere for these," she said. "They're Clarissa's. She wanted them for her trip." Sara's younger half-sister, Clarissa, had just flown to Chicago for a short vacation.

"How'd you end up with them?"

"Clarissa borrowed the coat."

I thought about Clarissa for a moment too long. "I wonder how her trip's going," I said.

"Ask her when she gets back." Sara looked at me frigidly.

"When exactly would I do that?" I rarely spoke to Clarissa, unless she was tagging along with Sara for drinks at the TimeWarp, which she rarely did.

"Dinner at my dad's house on Sunday? Tell me you didn't forget."

I had it on my calendar, so I would have seen it. But I had, in fact, completely forgotten. "What's the occasion again?"

"There's no occasion. My dad just wants to show off, as usual. Probably some obscure new recipe or weird cut of meat. He's sick of showing off to the other doctors, so it's just us this time. But don't worry, it'll be fun. Clarissa will play the piano. Dad'll get tipsy. Conversation will get heated. You know, the usual."

Sara had more to say. Her eyes revealed that. But it would have to wait. "Gotta go," she said. She stepped backward toward the open door and looked past me toward the windows. Her eyes seemed to breathe in and out. Cryptically, she snapped her fingers. My heart jumped when I thought maybe she was seeing my mother for the first time. I looked over my shoulder. Nothing there but the two tall windows, the red walls, and the shitty western light that I dreaded to paint by. I looked back. Sara had slipped out the door, silent as an unopened letter.

The morning was hazy and wet, my mother had disappeared into it, Sara was gone, and I was alone with my work. After a morning like that, I knew it would be hard to begin painting, but I had no choice. I walked over to the window. March in Minneapolis can be tortuously cold, blustery, and generally miserable, with absurd accumulations of snow that in more normal climes would be spring rain. But this day was, at least, merely overcast and depressing. Little snow remained. I scanned the street for signs of my mother, or Sara, but saw neither. I turned back and faced my easel.

My plan for the day was to begin another painting. I was desperately behind schedule for my upcoming exhibition. In just three weeks I would need at least five more finished paintings for my first show at Perimeter Gallery. I managed to land the show on the strength of just a few paintings along with a personal recommendation from my former professor, Vernon Nilsson, one of the gallery's biggest draws. Still, if my paintings weren't all ringers, my first show would also be my last.

I had set a nearly blank canvas on my easel the night before in hopes of working a bit in the middle of the night, as I often did. But, miraculously, I had stayed asleep right up until Pigeonhole came home. Now, my box of paints sat wide open, a gaping mouth threatening me like a lion baring its teeth. I pulled out several tubes of alkyd paint in various colors. On my palette, I squeezed out the paint I needed to get started, and for a few minutes, I just stared at the colors, mixing them together in my mind, thinking about the tones of shadow and light I was hoping to create. Finally, beneath the twilight sky I had painted the day before, I roughed-in the image of a gray, aluminum-sided suburban split-level house with an attached two-car garage. In the driveway I sketched in a red tricycle and a white house cat. The lawn was in need of mowing, and the few trees and shrubs in the yard had only recently been planted.

A dull suburban scene such as this was a common motif for me. But once an image of this kind neared completion, I would begin the process of destroying what I had just created. Usually, it was by fire. I would paint smoke and flames, setting fire to the house or garage or car, or all of it, and letting it all burn. Walls would crumble, roofs collapse, gas tanks explode, and so on, until the entire scene became a disaster. In this particular case, I moved quickly to the aftermath. Billows of smoke came from the now burned-out car that sat inside the garage. The grass was singed, the trees charred, the siding melted. The cat, the lone apparent survivor, simply looked on.

After five hours and several cups of coffee, I was nearly finished with the painting. For me, this was amazing progress. As I took a break and sat on the edge of my bed, my mind drifted to the many ways in which my mother had appeared to me. Often, she would descend from above, gracefully floating down through the ceiling, hovering in front of me. Sometimes she would materialize in a puff of smoke, as if by wizardry. I never knew if I was seeing something supernatural or if I was suffering the same form of hallucinations my mother experienced in her short life. More than once I had seen her passing by on a city bus, often the only passenger, making me wonder if I was hallucinating the entire bus itself. I wondered if I was ever truly alone, or if she was always there watching me from some hidden vantage point.

The visions I had, however, did help me grasp my paint brush that much tighter and for that much longer. In some sense, I held onto it for dear life. If I loosened my grip, my mother might have snatched the brush from me and taken over, giving me a lesson as if I were still a child, one she seemed to believe couldn't make progress without her. Sometimes my fingers ached after clutching the brush so tightly for so many hours at a time. Sometimes I dropped the brush in exhaustion. Only then was I willing to give up and accept the inevitable—that my mother would take up the brush and work on my paintings in my stead. My debt to her then continued to accrue, her otherworldly ability the only thing that could rescue me from the corner I had painted myself into. If it weren't for her, I would never have gotten my first show, and if I had known how much I needed her to complete the work, I'm sure I would have resisted her less, if at all. As it was, I wanted to at least prove to myself, and to her, what I was capable of without her help.

At five o'clock Sara texted saying she'd be over at six-thirty. She arrived at eight, unlocking the door on her own, striding past me at my easel, straight to the bed at the far side of the room. She appeared to be a little drunk, and as such, her usual late-day agitation was not on display. Instead, she was quiet and still. She sat on the bed and looked up at the ceiling fan as I went to the nightstand for the oil she liked me to massage into her skin.

"Not tonight," she said as she fell back onto the pillows. I sat down next to her. I wanted to ask her what the matter was, what the matter always was, but I took her cue and remained silent. "Put on some music," she said. I knew what this meant. I grabbed my phone to activate the Bluetooth speaker on my nightstand, and she said, "No, the turntable." I got up and powered on my old stereo. I put on an old Joni Mitchell record, Sara's favorite, *Hejira*. Sara wiggled out of her jeans. "See if you can last for the whole side," she said. I nodded. As the music played and we began to kiss, my mind wandered, as it often did. In fact, my detachment from sex was often strangely pronounced, but Sara said she liked it that way. She called it "wanderlust."

In the middle of "A Strange Boy," Sara began to climax. Just then, Pigeonhole, as if waiting in the wings, turned on his amp and began to play, with Tanya accompanying him on the bongo drums. When it was over, I rolled back onto the pillows and stared up at the ceiling. Pigeonhole stopped playing briefly, presumably to shoot up or swallow a mouthful of pills. After a moment he began playing again with a renewed fervor. I wasn't sure what possessed me, but I got up, grabbed my robe, and stormed down the hall. I pounded on the star. Glitter fell, dusting my toes. The unlocked door swung open on its aging hinges.

Pigeonhole stood stiffly in a pair of black leather pants, his hair alive with frizz and his guitar slung low. He wore a plastic armored breastplate and a horned, polished steel Viking helmet. Tufts of foam collected along his lips. A spiked leather collar gripped his neck. Two guitar picks jutted from between his teeth like fangs.

Tanya, apparently now in a stupor, was curled up on the floor in a chintzy blouse and jodhpurs, cradling the slingshot Pigeonhole used to shoot at cockroaches from across the room. An open bottle of Jack Daniels—pink lipstick at the rim—was within reach should she come to, but that didn't seem likely. A typical night.

"Harry, can you just unplug for once?"

"I never unplug. And stop calling me that. Use my stage name."

"Fine. Pigeonhole, if you quit for the night, just this once, I will tear up my vintage poster of Prince and the Revolution. The one you hate."

He contemplated my offer while churning out a deluge of notes. "No deal," he finally said. "Although I am tempted by the visual." He glanced back at his life-sized cardboard cutout of Eddie Van Halen.

"Because you're jealous of Prince," I said. "Because he was better than you."

He stopped playing and pointed his middle finger at me. "I am not jealous of that purple fucker!" He walked over to Tanya, picked up the slingshot, and put his guitar pick into the pouch. He pulled the bands back tight and fired the pick at me. It glanced off my forehead, nearly weightless, but it stung. Laughing maniacally, he turned up his amp, stomped on an effect pedal, and began playing the guitar with his teeth.

Enough, I thought. More than enough. I would do what I had to do. I picked up the cardboard Eddie and carried it to the door. Eddie was smiling at me, blissfully unaware of what was about to happen. I walked into the hallway and stood at the top of the stairs. Cold March air filled the stairwell from the leaky door below. I cocked Eddie back and torpedoed him down, watching him fall to the floor like a dead bird. He landed face up, still smiling of course, but somehow the smile now seemed less oblivious.

Pigeonhole stumbled into the hallway and threw off his guitar. Still connected to the amplifier, the guitar landed on the wooden floor with the sound of a thousand smashed cuckoo clocks. Moving faster than I thought possible, Pigeonhole lunged past me and into the stairwell. Though I stood frozen, there would have been no stopping him. He moved with the quickness and inevitability of a man falling in love, or—even more quickly and more inevitably—a man falling out of love. He dove headfirst down the stairs screaming "Eddie!" at the top of his lungs. He landed on his head halfway down, toppled over himself, and crashed on top of his cutout idol.

I stood frozen in disbelief. Tanya, roused by the clangor, burst into the hallway and ran past me nearly as quickly as Pigeonhole had. But somehow, unlike Pigeonhole, she managed to wobble her way down the stairs without injuring herself in the process.

"What the fuck did you do?" she slurred. I wasn't sure which of us she meant. I followed her to the bottom of the stairs. Pigeonhole was breathing, but his body was limp. My hope that he was merely unconscious and not seriously injured. My hope appeared to become a reality when Tanya slapped him and he woke up.

Tanya looked up, not quite at me, just vaguely upward. "Go away!" she yelled in a tone so dead that it was again unclear which one of us she was speaking to. She must have realized this when I didn't move. She then pointed at me and repeated herself. I wasn't going to make her do it again. I turned and headed up the stairs, feeling both relieved and, I had to admit at the time, a little vindicated.

As I passed Pigeonhole's open door, I spotted the slingshot. I went in and picked it up, put it on my wrist, pinched the empty pouch, and pulled the straps back. I would need this someday, I thought. I wasn't sure for what, but somehow I knew. And there was something about being hit by the slingshot that made me feel entitled to it. I took it back to my apartment, fully aware that I had just made a cold and bizarre emotional turn from which I might never recover.

"Wow, he stopped," Sara said as I walked in. "What'd you do, threaten him with his own slingshot?"

"Not exactly."

"Then what are you doing with that thing?"

"Nothing. It's mine now." I stashed it under my bed, moved to the window, and opened it wide.

"What the hell was all that racket anyway?"

"Something happened," I said. "Pigeonhole ..." I paused not knowing exactly how to relate what had happened. "... fell down the stairs. I mean he threw himself down the stairs. Actually, I don't really know what happened."

Sara got out of bed and went into the hallway to see for herself. A moment later she returned. "Oh my God!" she stage-whispered. "How the fuck did that happen?"

"No idea. All I did was throw that stupid cardboard Eddie Van Halen down the stairs, and he went flying after it."

"So it was your fault?"

"My fault? I didn't push him. He did it to himself. And why are you whispering?"

"Eddie was his idol. How would you like it if someone chucked all your paintings out the window?"

"Well, I wouldn't jump out after them."

"Of course you would."

"So?"

"So have some compassion!"

"It's his own fault!"

Her eyes stared at me unmovingly, as if she wasn't sure who I was, as if I were someone from her distant past who she couldn't quite recognize. Her fists were clenched. She tapped her foot jerkily, her still-stockinged legs throbbing like two black keys on a player piano. She threw up her hands, dressed quickly, and went down to check on Pigeonhole and Tanya.

I kept an eye on the street until the police and an ambulance arrived. One of the police officers, bellowing as if he wanted the entire building to overhear, explained to the paramedics that Pigeonhole was destined to end up in jail, hospitalized, or dead. "It was only a matter of time," he asserted. Thank God, I thought, for Pigeonhole's many run-ins with the law. I was off the hook.

As they rolled Pigeonhole on a gurney into a waiting ambulance, I took a final inventory of the scene playing out below: one fire truck, two police cars, an ambulance, three paramedics, four cops, a firefighter, Sara, and Tanya. There was only one person missing, I told myself. I leaned out the window and looked straight down. There on the sidewalk stood my dead mother, looking back up at me.

CHAPTER 2

IT WAS EARLY spring, barely into April, when my life ended and my death began. That terrible day started much like any other. Saturday morning came, and as usual I took my medication before William woke up. I made coffee for myself, squeezed two oranges for William, and watched the morning news on TV. But by late morning my mind had given me an instruction, one I knew deep down I would receive eventually: I was to bring William to his grandmother's, return home, and set fire to our house with myself inside it. At the time, it seemed sensible. Like a routine chore. I was just following the script, as I so often did, not arguing with myself, not checking myself against any neutral measure of right and wrong.

I waited until after breakfast to tell William I needed to take him to my mother's house. I hadn't prepared a proper excuse. "Get some books and games together. And bring a few of your favorite toys. Your grandma likes Boggle. Bring that." I'd packed him a small suitcase and had that in my car already. Enough clothes and toiletries for a week, no more. It was all I could manage.

William was confused. "I don't want to go."

"Your grandmother is expecting you," I lied. I hadn't even called her. "She has a surprise for you."

"What is it?"

"I can't tell you. It's a surprise."

"I hate those."

"You'll like this one. It's something you'll remember forever."

I don't know why I said that. I knew it was cruel, something no mother should say to her child on their last day together. Maybe I needed to inflict a certain amount of cruelty to keep my plan from careening off the tracks. Or maybe I knew it would get me what I wanted, what I needed: William in the car, ready to go. It did.

Though my mother was not expecting us, she was rather delighted with the situation. The suitcase concerned her, but what choice did she have? I handed it to her, kissed William on the cheek, and drove off. On the way home, my mind floated above me like a migratory bird. Does a bird argue against its predetermined course? Or does it simply follow the voice inside its head that tells it where to fly next? My thoughts were not with my son or what might become of him. My thoughts were not really with myself either. My thoughts were not even my own. They just were.

On the way home I stopped at an art supply store and purchased a full gallon can of turpentine. The clerk was so young, closer to my son's age than to mine. Would he think of me when he saw our house on the news? Probably not. He had no idea the devastation he was helping to conjure. I hoped he would never make the connection.

"Will there be anything else?" he asked. "Paints? Brushes? Canvases?"

"That won't be necessary."

Five minutes later, I pulled into the garage and pushed the button to close the garage door for the last time. I watched the door drop like a curtain coming down in an empty theater. Entering the house, I scanned the room, again for the final time, or so I thought. Was this really going to work? Was this enough turpentine? What if it wasn't? A voice told me that it was. I set the turpentine down, went to the kitchen, and opened the refrigerator. Nothing unusual in there. I had forgotten to buy milk. The oranges were starting to get soft. I left the door open. Why bother to close it? I went into William's room, a mistake. I made his bed, fluffed the pillows, put a few of his strewn toys away. I dragged the wooden rocking chair, where I had sat and read to him for so many years, out of his bedroom and into the middle of the living room.

After sitting in the rocker for a moment, I got up and splashed turpentine on the chair and carpet. The smell was startlingly strong. Things were getting serious now, there was no denying that. After soaking the couch and drapes, I made a trail down the stairs and found myself staring at the record player. I couldn't help but turn it on. The record on the turntable was a junk store find, a classic country compilation I liked. The first track was "Love Is Where You Find It," by Loretta Lynn and Conway Twitty. As it spun, I poured turpentine on top of the record, causing the needle to slide across the grooves. I had to flip it over. The first track on the other side, by George Jones and Tammy Wynette, was their hit "We're Gonna Hold On." Were we? Did they? No, and no. And I knew that no song, no matter how many times it could make a mother cry, was going to save me now.

I kept a bar downstairs and fixed myself a drink. There were pills as well, which I kept hidden in the basement where William would never find them. I was becoming a cold, dead bird, no longer migrating, my days in flight behind me. I poured turpentine on my dress, my arms, my hair. I sat down inside a small meditation pyramid I had constructed out of slats of wood and sheets of clear plastic. I had spent hours and hours inside that pyramid, hoping that somehow it would direct my thoughts away from this very moment. Another failure. I pulled the box of matches from my pocket. I held a match out and studied the red tip. The hardest part would be striking the match with enough force for it to catch fire. I was trembling. There was, I admit, a moment when I thought I couldn't go through with it. But I realized soon enough that I was in no condition to clean up all the turpentine, and certainly not by myself. Asking for help would mean I'd end up in a psych ward—still alive but separated from William. That somehow seemed worse than death.

I dragged the match head across the strike plate. That my arm was suddenly on fire was the strangest sensation. Before the heat came, there was a whoosh that ate up half the oxygen in the room. I let out a scream. Not from terror or pain. It was relief. It had been a long time since I had felt any such sense of tranquility. There was no going back.

The room was now engulfed in fire. The vinyl records I cherished were burning before me. Soon the music stopped with the burst of a vacuum tube. Then I passed out, either from lack of oxygen or from pain or both. As I slipped away, the last thought I had was a feeling of accomplishment. I had done it. My life was over.

But, though my life was indeed over, I would soon find out that death wasn't the end. The next thing I knew I was standing inside the pyramid. My heart had stopped beating—an alarming state of being, like free-falling but going nowhere. My hands were charred kindling, and my nails were encrusted with ash. I could sense—but for some reason could not hear—the fire consuming the house around me. Unable to see more than a few feet in any direction, I stepped out of the blazing pyramid. With my charred hands, I felt for the wall next to the stairs. Though it was certainly hot, to me it was cool to the touch, as everything would be from then on. With my palms pressed against the wall, I could feel fire roaring above me. I followed the wall to the stairs and ascended.

I exited the house through the back door. By this time, it was dusk. I must have spent half the day asleep before I struck the match, but I had no recollection of time. I entered the yard as some of my neighbors were desperately looking in the windows, trying to see if anyone was home. The lights of a fire truck approaching lit the smoke alternately red and white. There may have been sirens, but if there were, I could not hear them. The roof collapsed before the firefighters managed to hook up the hoses. They weren't going to save the house, that much was clear. Less clear was how on earth I was still there to see the results of my terrible handiwork.

Now, years later, the voices are gone, but I'm still here, still wandering in and out of my son's life like the mother I never could have been when I was alive.

CHAPTER 3

THE FOLLOWING WEEK was dedicated entirely to painting. After several grueling days, I had made significant progress. But on this particular day, after spending ten hours on the same painting, I was left with little to show for my efforts other than stiff fingers from gripping the brush too tightly and for too long. That evening I was scheduled to meet Sara at her father's house for dinner. It would have been a relief to finish the painting before I needed to get cleaned up, but there was not enough time. At six o'clock I tugged off my old work boots and exchanged my paint-stained coveralls for a bright orange oxford and my only decent pair of pants—a pair of dun-colored H&M corduroys, a brand I despised for its banality until it started show up at Goodwill dirt cheap. As I put my boots back on, I gazed at the painting. I felt it would look better facing the wall. I removed it from the easel and set a fresh, primed canvas in its place for later. A puddle of linseed oil spilled on the floor next to the easel had attracted and trapped a small, pale cockroach. I left it there.

I made my way down the hallway to the bathroom. The cardboard Eddie had returned. He stood in the bathtub, smiling beneath the showerhead as if ready to rinse the hair gel out of his mullet. Why he was in the bathroom, I had no idea. Maybe Tanya brought him inside after the incident. As I brushed my teeth, squinting in the fluorescent light, I studied the lines of mildew that wound their way around the inside of the antique tub like the rings of an ancient sequoia. It had been Pigeonhole's turn to clean the bathroom for months. I tried to forget that regrettable fact as I turned off the light and headed downstairs.

On my fifth try, my car, an old Volvo 240 wagon, finally started. I checked the gas gauge. I had maybe two gallons, just enough to drive the twenty miles due west from Minneapolis to the suburb of Deephaven, where Sara and Clarissa had grown up and where their father still lived. Since its early days, the tiny hamlet (as the obnoxiously self-aware residents so quaintly termed it) had been quiet and comfortable—rich, but not too rich. Sara's father, Dr. Anders Karlsen, born in Duluth but raised, in his words, in a Hibbing iron mine, liked to show off a bit, but he wasn't showy in a crass way. He was unwilling to sell his house and move (as more than a few of the neighbors had) when an unsightly gas station was constructed down the block in the early 1990s. At the time it was a Clark. Later it became an Amoco, and finally a BP. The ghastly green-and-yellow sign ablaze all night kept the crass rich buried farther west, closer to the shores of Lake Minnetonka.

Sara's father came to Minneapolis as a young man to attend the University of Minnesota School of Medicine and eventually became a reconstructive surgeon known throughout the Midwest for successfully reattaching the arms of a sixteen-year-old Minnesota farm boy who had them torn off in a misguided but well-meaning attempt to dislodge a turtle from a thresher. TV stations throughout the region had covered the surgery and the many months of recovery. The boy's reattached arms were slightly shorter than before, and he appeared to be constantly shrugging his shoulders in disbelief. But, after much physical therapy, chronic digit numbness, endless videos showing him fumbling through the simple tasks of daily life—along with a certain communal if taciturn Midwestern faith—his fingers had begun to re-learn the once familiar motions he had so effortlessly memorized as a child: the zip, the tuck, the button, the snap. He could perform them all, if clumsily. Over time, his proficiency became nearly indistinguishable from that of his former self, or anyone else for that matter. He went on to marry his high school sweetheart and later had a son of his own. He was, and remains, Dr. Karslen's masterpiece—a work of medical art no sane surgeon would ever want the opportunity to rival.

Dr. Karlsen's wife, Dr. Shelley Harrison, born in Rochester, Minnesota, had also been a medical doctor. She studied at Johns Hopkins and met her husband just after medical school when traveling in South America with the Peace Corps. They both wanted to live and practice in their home state—though exactly where was up for debate as Dr. Karlsen did not favor the Mayo Clinic, where his father had died of a grand mal seizure at the age of forty-one. A compromise was reached—they would both practice at the University of Minnesota Hospital and Clinic—and soon they were married. In fact, they were married twice—once in an elaborate Catholic ceremony at the cathedral in St. Paul and once again in a decidedly less romantic ceremony after a brief, unceremonious divorce. She was pregnant both times. Their first baby was Sara. The second, three years later, was Clarissa. The second father, however, was not Dr. Karlsen. It was another doctor, a psychologist who Dr. Nilsson had been seeing, as a patient no less. He wanted an abortion. She didn't. Eventually, Dr. Karlsen claimed Clarissa as his legal daughter, and after that, the situation was rarely discussed. Sadly, just seven years later their mother succumbed to breast cancer. Sara told me her father honored her mother nightly over the years, often doting over an old photograph of her while pouring her glass of sherry along with one for himself. This was tolerated, but only just, by his teenage daughters at the time.

I parked a few doors down from the Karlsen house to avoid any embarrassment for them and for myself. My thirty-year-old Volvo had lost several pounds to rust and missing parts, but it was all I could afford—my money, like my time, a commodity I neither cherished nor paid attention to. As I got out of my car, the drips of paint on my shabby boots reminded me that I couldn't leave that embarrassment entirely behind. Shabby things look that much shabbier in a posh suburb. I marched up the walk, rang the doorbell, and waited. After thirty long suburban seconds, Clarissa opened the inner door and peered at me through the screen door.

"Good evening, William," she said in a voice of mock formality. "Dinner's not ready yet." She did not open the screen door. Clarissa, at twenty-six but somehow appearing anywhere between twenty and fifty, wore her wavy auburn hair in a bun twisted neatly atop her head. Unlike Sara, Clarissa rarely wore makeup. But that night she had applied dark lipstick and heavy eyeliner. That, combined with the fancy black dinner dress and the blurring effect of the screen, forced me to look twice to be sure who it was.

"Dinner's never ready when you get to a dinner party," I said. "You have to talk first."

"This isn't a dinner party. It's just us and you," she said. "You look pale."

"I've been painting."

"Come in. The door's not locked."

I opened the screen door and stepped in. "Where's Sara?"

"She went to get mint jelly." Clarissa scrunched up her nose. "For the pork roast."

"You should've called me," I said. "I could've stopped on the way."

"My dad thought you might be too broke," she said in a tone suggesting she concurred.

"I can afford mint jelly," I said, wondering if it were actually true. I took off my boots. We walked up the half-flight of stairs to the living room. Clarissa sat at the piano and began paging through sheet music. I could hear Dr. Karlsen rummaging around in the kitchen.

The Karlsen house had been built in the 1960s and was fully remodeled in the 1990s a few years after they moved in. It was due for another go-around, but Dr. Karlsen didn't want to spend the money. He was, in his words, "saving for retirement." Sara would surely need tuition money once she decided to take the LSAT and apply to law schools, which was Dr. Karlsen's plan for her. Sara's degree in art history "wasn't cutting it," again, his words. Then there was Clarissa, who was currently in graduate school part time pursuing an MBA. So many expenses. But in truth, Dr. Karlsen had more money than he knew what to do with.

Without leaving the kitchen, Dr. Karlsen said, "Good evening, William," in his own version of mock formality, which was almost indistinguishable from actual formality. Maybe to him they were the same thing.

"Good evening, Dr. K," I said. "I mean, Dr. Karlsen."

"Dr. K is fine," he assured me.

"Dr. K it is," I said. I bowed slightly, attempting a physical gesture of pseudo formality, though he could not see me from where I stood in the middle of the living room. The split-level house had an open floor plan, but the kitchen was separated by a brick wall that reached more than ten feet in height, ending just short of the vaulted ceiling. The dining room adjoined the living room, divided only by the baby grand piano where Clarissa now sat.

"We were just picking out some sheet music for Clarissa to entertain us with before dinner," he said. "Do you like Philip Glass?"

"Glass? I love Glass," I said. "Speaking of glass, that's a beautiful mirror on the dining room wall over there. Is it new?"

"It is new," Dr. Karlsen said. "Antique, that is, but new to us."

"It's Aegean glass," Clarissa added.

"Wow, Aegean glass," I said. "Can you beat that?"

"How about 'Einstein on the Beach' for piano, Clarissa?" Dr. Karlsen asked from the kitchen with obvious glee. He must have been working on something, or he would have come out to greet me. "Do you think you can manage that for us?"

"I played it at one of my recitals in high school. And I can still read," she said, pointing to the sheet music in front of her. "And you asked me to prepare it for tonight. So, yeah." She began to warm up.

"Those lessons cost me fucking a fortune," Dr. Karlsen said, possibly to no one in particular. "Would you like something to drink, William? We have Trinity spring water, a high-tech Oregon merlot, and Diet Coke."

"I'll try the merlot, please." I added the "please" because I always tried to be as polite as possible whenever I was around Dr. Karlsen. It wasn't just me trying to look good in his eyes. In some sense, I felt it was my duty to make white millennial men seem better than we actually are.

Finally, Dr. Karlsen paraded into the living room wearing full chef regalia—white coat, puffy hat, checkerboard apron. In one hand he wielded a giant four-pronged fork, and in the other he held a glass of red wine, which he handed to me.

"The vineyard is in Oregon, but the family is French, don'tcha know," he said, jacking up his Minnesota accent.

"Where's your coat, William?" he asked, looking around the room. "You trying to catch a cold?" He pointed the fork at me.

"No," I said. "It's unseasonably warm out today, so I didn't need one."

"Oh, come on now. It's still March, you know. Lambs. Lions. Coats! Or so they say." He lowered the fork and returned to the kitchen just as Sara arrived.

She threw open the door and sprinted up the stairs. She wore a high-collared black dress, long and sleeveless, with red floral embroidery. Also no coat, though her outfit looked like she could have used one. In one hand she held a small purse, and in the other she clutched a plastic bag tied in a little bundle.

"They didn't have mint jelly at G. Harper's," she said, "so I stole these jelly packets from that rib place on Minnestra Street." For some reason she handed me the bag.

"That's ingenious," Clarissa said, continuing to play as if it were nothing but background music. "You're a regular Martha Stewart." She wobbled her head a little in time with the music, now playing a bit louder.

"As usual," Sara said, "that makes absolutely no sense."

Sara leaned in to kiss my cheek. I braced myself, not knowing what to expect. Sometimes she would hit me with a gentle peck, movie star style, while other times she would practically latch on like a lamprey, sucking the life force right out of my face. This time it was the former, followed by a fake smile, also movie star style. Hard to blame her after what we went through the week before. Sara then twirled around and strode down the hallway to the bathroom.

I took a deep breath and sipped my wine. Clarissa was playing her well-rehearsed music beautifully. She held long, repeating bass notes with her left hand while delicately plucking a melody of sorts with her right. She began to mumble some lyrics I couldn't make out. Maybe the mumbling was part of the piece. I had heard it once before on the radio when I was in college, but had not given it much thought since. Hearing it this way made me wish I had.

"It's nice to hear something besides electric guitar shredding for a change," I said. "Though I haven't had to worry about that since last week."

"I heard about that," Clarissa said, missing a note or two from what I could tell. "Maybe you should elaborate over dinner."

I choked a bit on my wine. "Sorry, no. It's not an appropriate topic for dinner conversation. Unless," I added, "you all want to puke."

Dr. Karlsen leaned out the kitchen door and raised an amateur actor's eyebrow in reaction to my use of the word "puke." He looked a bit like the Swedish Chef from *The Muppet Show:* mustache, bushy eyebrows, red bulb nose, everything but the bow tie. He probably had one close at hand.

Sara returned to the living room wearing a fresh coat of makeup. She was rubbing her bare shoulders as if to warm up, but it also looked like she was about to cast a spell of some kind. One involving me, no doubt.

"You didn't call all week?" she admonished. "I was getting worried." Her tone was more pissed than worried, but her father's presence tempered her choice of words.

"My show is coming up fast."

"Meaning no calls? Not even me?"

"The entire week was a blur."

"I was going to stop by with dinner, but you didn't answer my texts."

"You have a key."

Sara and Clarissa both grimaced. Cohabitation of any kind was not approved of, nor discussed, in the presence of the almost maniacally protective Dr. Karlsen. Sara and I also never discussed it much, in particular because she hated my apartment. But I refused to sleep at hers more than a few times a month because my insomnia had only one cure: getting up and painting in the middle of the night. I told Sara it was insomnia, anyway. What it really was was my mother waking me up, putting a brush in my hand, telling me to get back to work. Not an easy thing to sleep through.

Dr. Karlsen stepped from the kitchen to the dining room with a tray full of salads. He invited us to sit down at the table. He placed one of the salads in front of me and continued around the table as adeptly as a seasoned waiter. The vinaigrette, though served in a crystal decanter, was clearly store-bought, an unusual choice for Dr. Karlsen, who seldom took shortcuts. He had also forgotten the mint jelly. I wondered if he had been held up at the hospital.

I chewed the salad greens as slowly as I could, admitting to myself that these kinds of dinners intimidated me. Sara's father had money, status, class. His daughters were intelligent and beautiful. I, by contrast, was nearly destitute, had made the worst of an average college education, and was, practically speaking, a complete failure—possibly as an artist, but almost certainly as a human being. The fact that I ate slowly, as if entirely for pleasure, was my single advantage.

"William, have you found a new place to live? I know you've been searching." Dr. Karlsen certainly knew I couldn't afford anything better, though I had spoken previously of my desire to move.

"I'm still waiting for my housing assignment from the government," I said.

"Ah, political humor," he said. "Love it."

"I'm not sure where you're going with that one," Sara said.

"We never discuss politics at the dinner table," Clarissa said.

"I was kidding," I insisted.

"Or religion," she added with a tap of a fingernail on the edge of her plate.

Dr. Karlsen rolled his eyes as he pulled his fork from his mouth, scraping the tines across his teeth.

"The fact is I'll never find a 1,500-square-foot studio apartment for $700 a month, unless I move to Ames, Iowa, or somewhere even more boring. I need all that wall space for my paintings."

"Speaking of walls, William," Dr. Karlsen said, changing the subject, "I have a favor to ask."

"A favor?" I was a little surprised and also a little worried.

"I'm planning to paint my home office, and I know you, as an artist, have an eye for color. I'm looking for a color—how can I put this?—a color so sublime that even if I sell the house someday, I'll want to take my office with me. Make sense?"

I scratched my forehead.

"Good. I'll pay you a consultation fee of $200, besides providing you with this meal, which I notice you're barely touching so far."

"I accept the challenge," I said, "of finding a color sublime enough to take with you when you move, or whatever that was." Truth be told, I couldn't possibly have said no. Not merely because he was asking in front of Sara and Clarissa, but because for $200, I would have painted his office myself.

"Glad to hear you're on board," he said. "Or whatever that was. Now eat! Because the best part has yet to be reckoned with."

Dr. Karlsen took great pleasure in his elaborate meals. Cooking was his only pastime, other than watching European soccer matches online. He was a surgeon first and foremost. It was his identity, whether he was on a picnic, mowing his lawn, paying devotion to his late wife, or, I presumed, preparing an elegant meal. He often decoratively carved carrots with an old scalpel he had brought home early in his career after a particularly difficult but successful procedure.

I was not quite done with my salad when Dr. Karlsen stood up and started collecting all the plates. "Now, my pretties," he said, "the moment I hope you've all been waiting for, as I have." He carried the plates into the kitchen.

I heard the oven door open, followed by a moan of satisfaction. A minute later, Dr. Karlsen carried in a platter that held an elaborately garnished roast, his latest masterpiece.

"Roast pork with fennel, garlic, and herbs. Why simply eat, when one can truly dine?"

"Where'd you get the recipe?" Clarissa asked.

"*The New York Times*?" Sara asked.

"It was your mother's recipe," Dr. Karlsen said solemnly. He sliced the roast deftly with a shimmer stainless-steel blade. "This is one of the largest hand tools in modern medicine," he said. "I ordered it from Lithuania especially for the kitchen. At one time, not so long ago in terms of science, this type of blade was used to prepare a limb for amputation. William, pass me your plate."

I did, and he gave me two thick slices. "I have a wonderful baguette warming in the oven, as well as some braised onions, steamed potatoes, and, of course, the mint jelly Sara picked up for us from … Tubby's." Dr. Karlsen filled everyone's plates. "This is called a French cut, bones intact. I always pick it up fresh from the butcher the same morning. I rub the roast with Italian olive oil. Then, sea salt and pepper, fennel and garlic. All day long it sits. No refrigeration! Then, into the oven for just twenty-five minutes."

I tried to think of something to say, but I couldn't form words while attempting to bear the thought of eating a rare pork roast, let alone one so alarmingly rare. Just then,

Clarissa piped up: "William, have you seen the new painting show at the Walker?"

"*Nine Lives*? Yes, I went to the opening. And I've seen it twice since then," I said.

"What did you think?"

"I'm still thinking about it. But I'm an artist, not a critic."

"What's an 'art critic' anyway?" Clarissa asked, using air quotes. "Is it just a failed artist who feels the need to cast others down to even lower levels of dejection than they themselves?"

"Clarissa, that's stupid," Sara blurted.

"Actually, Clarissa's pretty much right," I said. Clarissa looked rapt; Sara, miffed. "Critics just want to see if they can get artists to jump through meaningless hoop after meaningless hoop. And, for whatever reason, artists trip all over themselves to oblige. Even the famous ones."

"All except Julian Schnabel," Clarissa said. "He's another story entirely."

"Why Schnabel?" I asked. He had a big purple painting in the exhibition. Clarissa must have seen it. Or at least read about it.

"He does what he wants," she said. "Painting, directing films, surfing. Not a hoop-jumper."

"'Schnabel' is, as you might know," Dr. Karlsen said, "the German word for 'schnoz.'" He pointed to his nose.

"Not exactly, Dad," Clarissa said. "It means beak."

"How do you know that?" he asked.

"I read it somewhere," she said.

"I guess I'll have to Google that later," he said, removing his chef hat. "You're of German descent, aren't you, William?"

"On my mother's side," I said, wondering how he knew that. "But I never heard a word of German growing up."

"Well, you won't hear much here, either." He gestured to himself and his daughters. "You're surrounded by Scandinavians!"

"Story of my life," I said. "Could you please pass the wine?"

Clarissa handed me the bottle. As I took it, she left her hand on the bottle neck just long enough to give my knuckles a gentle caress. "Speaking of German," she said, turning to Sara, "remember that music store owner you dated a few years ago? Wasn't his name Einstein?"

"Stan," Sara said. "Stan Einstein. That was three years ago."

"Funny name," Clarissa said.

"I wouldn't call it funny," Dr. Karlsen said. "'Einstein' means 'one glass' in German. This I do know. And Philip Glass probably knows it too."

"Knows or knew?" Sara asked.

"Knows!" Clarissa said. "Unless he died this afternoon?"

Quick to change the subject yet again, Dr. Karlsen began talking about his latest procedure, a hand reconstruction. I sank into my chair and stared at my glass of wine as he spoke about tendons and nerve endings and skin grafts. I let my eyes go out of focus. I stared through the wine glass and past the dinner table, past Dr. Karlsen and the mirror behind him, through the sliding glass doors at the back of the house, across the yard, beyond the fence and hill, over the horizon, into outer space, and on and on into the galactic noise and infinite darkness.

I was shocked back into the room by an explosion from somewhere outside the house. The concussion was so great, it caused the Aegean glass mirror to fall off the dining room wall and Clarissa to knock the platter of gruesomely undercooked (though expertly prepared) pork onto the floor. The roast slid off the platter and bounced happily along the floorboards. At the same moment, the mirror hit the wainscoting, paused, then tipped forward, falling face down on the perfectly poised roast. To everyone's astonishment, the mirror did not break. A concussion from a second explosion shook the house again. No words were spoken. We all stood and headed down the half-flight of stairs to the door.

From the front yard we witnessed a giant fireball overtaking the setting sun, consuming what had been the service station at the end of the block.

"Oh my God, Clarks blew up!" shouted Dr. Karlsen. "I just had the BMW fixed there yesterday!" Dark smoke rose straight up from the station, enveloping the BP sign.

"It wasn't fixed," Sara corrected him. "They just rotated the tires. And it hasn't been Clarks for years." Even in this disastrous moment, Sara felt it necessary to make these distinctions.

"Don't be clever, Sara," Dr. Karlsen said. "This isn't one of your imaginary spots on *The Tonight Show*."

"I don't have imaginary spots on *The Tonight Show*!"

"Never mind," Dr. Karlsen said, waving her off. "I have to get closer, see if anyone needs help."

Dr. Karlsen walked briskly toward the flames, and we followed cautiously behind him. Nearer to the service station, people ran from their homes, clutching cats and infants. Parents united their families, if they could, or ran from yard to yard screaming for their children. Many people were on their phones, presumably making an unnecessary number of 911 calls. Others were taking videos of the blaze. Five minutes passed as we stared at the inferno. Sirens blared in the distance. I could not help wondering if my mother had anything to do with this.

Sara stood in front of me facing the fire. Her dark hair billowed and stabbed at the wind, her cheekbones burnished by the firelight. She must have felt me looking at her because she shifted her weight to her left hip and turned to face me. Sara looked just like her mother—I could tell from the pictures all over their house—and against this backdrop of incendiary commotion, she appeared to me more alluring than ever. I felt her searching my psyche, as if she were concluding, if only abstractly, that I might somehow have had a hand in this catastrophe. A tap on my shoulder from Clarissa brought me back to the present moment.

White ash began to fall like snow. A squirrel ran across the street and up into a tree. The fact that no one had emerged from the fire left me wondering if there were any casualties. Dr. Karlsen returned, having seen no one in need of first aid. "A miracle," he said. "The station is closed on Sundays." He guided us back to the house.

In the living room, Dr. Karlsen revealed a television set hidden beneath a cloth-covered table. He turned it on, changing the channel to a local station. A reporter was somehow already covering the scene live. The camera zoomed in for a closeup of the flames. What could possibly be happening so deep inside that burning place? Did it exist in any human sense? I turned away, toward the window. The sun had set, the blaze fully triumphant. Back on the TV screen, the flames grew and grew until—from deep within the raging fireball—the image of my dead mother appeared.

CHAPTER 4

I OFTEN WENT weeks without enduring visions of my mother. Sometimes longer. One year, an entire summer passed without seeing her at all. That was the summer before my first year of high school. At the time I thought my nightmare was finally over. But she probably just knew I needed to be alone. Maybe she was watching me the whole time, but I never saw her once that summer, never even felt her presence. But when she returned in the fall, it seemed as if she wanted something more than just to make her presence known. I never knew what she wanted, but a ghost (if that's the right word for her presence) must want something. To tell you something, or to change something, or for you to change something. But maybe that's wrong. Maybe ghosts just are.

I can easily imagine how, years ago, she had calculated how long it would be until I graduated high school. Ten years. Perhaps she had calculated the insurance money, the Social Security payments I would receive. She may have sat at her desk for the last time to pay a lingering bill or to balance her checkbook, not for my benefit, but merely for the sake of completeness. It's possible she conferred with the voices in her head, the labyrinth of characters, the competitive denizens of her mind. Did one voice take the lead in spite of the others, or were they all in agreement that the day had finally come? After that, an inventory. The furniture. Her bedding. Pictures. Clothing. Forty years' worth of kindling. Knowing my mother, she would have settled for nothing less than a complete account.

On to the essentials: turpentine, matches, alcohol, pills, a deck of tarot cards. And a place to send me, her only son, for the day. To her mother's house, where she stored all her paintings, safe and sound. Back at home, the doors and windows locked, blinds closed, shades pulled tight. The gas stove on, all four burners open full. And this business of a note? A note would only go up in flames with the rest of it. There would be no note.

By dusk, turpentine splashed in all corners of the house. A trail down the stairs, saturating the basement carpeting around the meditation rug. The old stereo, the glowing tubes, the shelves of records. All of it would burn. Before the match was struck, I imagine she put a record on. One of her beloved divas: Joni Mitchell, Joan Baez, Emmy Lou Harris, Aretha Franklin, Annie Lennox. Next, fuel on her arms and legs, and onto the floor where she sat in the lotus position, taking pills, drinking alcohol, the vodka burning on the way down, a prelude to her final act. For a moment, who knows, she might have considered disappearing, running off with some man, leaving the house to young William. Or she might have entertained the idea of having another child—a daughter this time, with any luck. Not another son. One was enough. Too many. But as the fantasies played themselves out, the pills took hold. Or the voices. Or both.

I can imagine our house, if it could still be called a house, consuming itself. In my mind I see her stand, walk upstairs and out the back door to the garden, no longer alive, but not quite dead, hidden behind a row of burning lilacs. There, listening to the willow tree pop and hiss in the heat, seeing the roof collapse, watching a bookcase tip, the precious volumes the last thing to catch fire. Did she see firefighters break down the front door? Did she laugh out loud at them, smoke billowing from her mouth, her voice rattling? Did she look down at the soil in her rose garden and see the hues she wished she could have captured in paint at that moment? The debris of her life behind her, years of wandering and waiting and haunting ahead. Perhaps.

The insurance money was enough to pay for a funeral and a new suit for me to wear to the wake. No father was listed on my birth certificate. There was nothing else. Social Security payments proved there was possibly someone, somewhere, who cared—some elected official or governmental bureaucrat who wrote a law designed to help people like me. Or maybe the law was about not having to care in the first place.

Still, I was lucky—if you could call it luck—to have in my possession every single painting my mother had left behind, all of them stashed away at my grandmother's house. Almost one hundred paintings in total, nearly every single one a masterpiece. She had been a nurse, but right after I was born, she quit to become a painter. She soon made a name for herself, not just in Minneapolis, but in galleries in Chicago and Santa Fe. But mere months after a show in New York had been planned, she succumbed to her disease. With no one to manage her estate other than her mother, her work faded from the scene just like that. Everyone moved on. Everyone but me.

My mother's favorite color? Red, of course. And from the beginning I became obsessed with that color—since the age of four when I came across an open, unguarded can of deck paint and painted myself completely red. I remember the feeling, the color seeming to enter me and course through my veins and come out through my eyes. When I was just starting grade school, my mother taught me about pigments, about the difference between cobalt blue and phthalo, about the way light reflects off a lead-white base, about cadmium and barium, about the heavy metals and the lighter ones—iron, especially iron—its oxide yielding a color resembling all the blood from a human body reduced to a single tube of paint. My mother taught me about color mixing, complements, underpainting, and glazing. So many lessons. I needed them more than I knew. But I discovered red for myself. My mother wasn't upset the day I painted myself red. On the contrary. That day, I believe, she saw—for the first time—that there was something I loved besides her.

CHAPTER 5

I FIRST MET Sara the summer before Pigeonhole's jump at an outdoor concert held in the sculpture garden at the Walker Art Center. It was the last week of June, the week Minneapolis descends into its annual vicious attack on personal outdoor space, the season known in normal climates as "summer." This is the season—maybe it lasts nine weeks?—into which literally every outdoor event must be jammed unless you want people to either freeze to death or file not exactly frivolous lawsuits claiming there should have been gas heaters or an unlimited supply of those weird foil jackets.

The oppressive Minnesota summer heat, the only other option, began early that year and with a vengeance. It was so hot I almost skipped the concert entirely. It was unusual for me to deliberately go to a crowded event in the first place, especially one so predictably sweaty and smelly. If I chose to venture out at all on a hot day, I preferred to wedge myself into the corner of a dark bar, alone with my drink, probably on the defensive lookout for my mother. In this case, something—let's call it luck—compelled me to attend, despite all my reservations. On my way out the door, I stuffed three bottles into my backpack: one of Jack Daniels, one of mosquito repellent, and one of water. I wasn't sure which would run out first.

I arrived just as My Morning Jacket was about to begin their set. Sara was facing the stage when I first saw her. I remember a sudden head rush, though I can't say I associated it with her at the time. The hot sun and the smell of bug spray were mingling with the Jack Daniels, and I was already lightheaded. When Sara turned around and glanced my way, everything froze—my thoughts, the band, the air—everything except the idea that my mother was suddenly right behind me and everyone could see her. Why else would a woman like Sara be looking so fervently in my direction? I turned around and checked behind me. My mother wasn't there, which really was no surprise. She almost never appeared to me in a crowd. I turned back. Sara laughed. She thought I was kidding. Little did she know I was dead serious.

I had no way of knowing at that moment if Sara was alone or with a dozen friends. But it didn't really matter. It was an outdoor concert in an urban sculpture park, and I was feeling electrified by the music of My Morning Jacket, and in spite of myself, I had already made a halfway decent joke. I had reason enough to walk up to her, so I did just that. As I approached, I could see that she was punishingly beautiful. As for me, I was coated in sweat, smelled of body odor and turpentine, and believed I was about to make a fool of myself, or worse. Then she leaned in and said, "Aren't you glad you came over?"

I definitely was. I pulled off my hat and dragged my hand across my sweaty forehead.

"There's paint all over your hands," she said.

I held them up. "I'm an artist." Impostor syndrome was making my head throb as I said this. "I mean, I'm a painter."

"I think I've seen your work around. Are you William Link?"

My knees nearly went out from underneath me. This had never happened to me before, and I didn't know what to say. The sun felt unbearably hot now. I was out of my element, that element being miserable obscurity, working alone in the middle of the night, wondering if my mother was going to show up and keep me company. I didn't know how to respond.

"I saw your stuff in the Jerome show at MCAD."

"How did you recognize me?" I was far from the only skinny, prematurely balding, bespectacled white dude within a stone's throw of that concert stage. A few of us were on the stage. We were everywhere—something I became acutely aware of at that moment.

"I was at the opening," she said. "I saw you there. You made a few remarks. And I remember your paintings. I loved all the color. Especially the red. So intense."

"I'm sorry, I don't remember much about that opening," I said, which was true.

"I was there with the deejay."

I didn't remember the deejay, nor did I remember her. But the fact that she remembered me—and my paintings— meant I had no choice but to immediately fall desperately in love with her, which is exactly what happened.

That night we went to her apartment, and even before the night was over, as immature as I knew it was, I told myself I never wanted to meet another woman again. I didn't know at the time what she saw in me, aside from remembering she liked my artwork. I was in a state of confusion the entire time. Before we fell asleep that night, I showed her a few of my new paintings on my phone. She told me they were brilliant. She had no idea that my mother was largely the reason for that.

A lot happened, quickly, but before I knew it, it was late summer and then early fall and then late fall, and we were still together. Totally unexpected. And it was spring before anything really started to go deeply wrong—wrong in the sense that my confused detachment had become the prominent factor in our relationship. But early on I had watched her diligently for any warning signs of ... what? Witchcraft? Espionage? Plans to run me through a wood-chipper? To be honest, I had no idea what I was on the alert for. Her apartment was full of books—lots of older, collectible books— stacked all over her apartment. She told me about hundreds more she had at her father's house. I found out later many had belonged to her mother. And she had tons of records, too—older country albums, '70s rock, '80s punk, '90s alternative. Nothing too obscure, but nothing banal. Stuff my own mother would have listened to. It felt like home somehow, I admit.

Many nights with Sara after that first night were wonderful, simple, just us being together, listening to music, reading, Sara scribbling in her journal, me working in my sketchbook or at the easel. It was like something from a movie, but a boring artsy movie, a movie where nothing much happens for far too long, sometimes for the whole movie. That being the point. They don't make too many movies like that anymore, but if they did, I'd know how the sequel goes.

Unfortunately, it became obvious that the sex, at least from Sara's perspective, was never that great (entirely my fault), but somehow Sara made it seem righteous in its predictability. The same moves, the same sounds, the same outcome. It became like clockwork, which suited me well enough, but for her it was like a ritual. We both fed off that sameness, as if it were a remedy for some obscure condition neither of us knew we had. And while she apparently thrived on the emotional distance I maintained, she occasionally managed to eke things out of me that I didn't know were there. I, on the other hand, attempted to hide the fact that it was easily the best sex of my life. I felt guilty, but I also felt that she wasn't merely accommodating me while hoping for something better later. There was more to it. Whatever it was, at first it gave me some hope, something I never had before, something I think hopeful people take for granted.

That first morning when she woke up, I had been sitting up in bed making sketches of her as she slept. She took a swig of the wine we had been drinking the night before and said, "Back to the grindstone already? Now I'm impressed." It started to rain about ten minutes later, just after I left her apartment, and I got soaked on the walk home. Maybe that was a sign of things to come, but if it was, I ignored it because she told me she wanted to see me again that night.

"Wear your coveralls," she said in a rather ominous tone.
"Why?"
"Because you're going to paint my portrait tonight."

Chapter 6

As a mother, my primary goal was to stay well enough to protect William—that is, to protect him from me. Maybe even to protect me from myself. But, over time, something took over, a terrible fixation that eclipsed William entirely. It came quietly at first, but then—as if a switch had been flipped—it was in control. Twisted thoughts, grisly voices, uncontrollable feelings. An impetus to destroy myself. But there was something more, something that went beyond all that. Although it was clearly an affliction of the mind, in my heart there was no longer any room for love, not even the love I felt for my own son, my own flesh and blood. The thing that mattered most to me had been taken away. And in its place? An abstract torrent of dread. In a sense, long before I ever struck that fateful match, I had already lost everything.

I never meant to hurt him. But my death wasn't about him. It wasn't even about me because I didn't know who I was anymore. I had forgotten myself. I was afraid I'd forget him, too. Forget not just guardianship, not just trust, not just love, but forget him entirely. And forgetting William would be far worse than anything death had to offer.

There was one day when I looked at my son and I didn't recognize him. He seemed like someone, or something, sinister, like a vampire or some kind of abhorrent beast. The feeling didn't last long. He began to speak, and the words I was hearing didn't match the sinister body, the fiendish look I thought I was seeing. The next thing I knew, my son was crying, embracing me. That's when I knew the end—my end—was near.

His father, by contrast, was someone I wanted to forget, but never did. He had been one of my patients at the hospital. A broken collarbone from a bar fight brought him in. A bout of pneumonia kept him there for another week. I violated every rule in the book when I slept with him, though it didn't happen at the hospital. He had been too unwell for that, and it's not something that would have even occurred to me. It happened months later, at a hotel downtown. I had not planned to find myself at a bar that night, but there I was. And there he was. And away we went. He was gone in the morning, along with all the cash in my purse. He never learned about William, and I kept it that way. I knew who he was, of course, and could have provided this information to William, but somehow I felt it was better to pretend his father never even existed.

After the fire, I did, in fact, wander off for a time, in a sense forgetting William. I spent years in hiding, existing neither in this world nor the next. I don't remember much about that time, but I knew that eventually I would return. When I finally did, I found my mother was nearly dead herself. Months of cancer treatment had ravaged her body and left her mind in a state of exhausted resignation. I was soon wandering the halls of the same hospital where I had once worked, watching the same doctors and nurses I had worked with taking care of my mother in her final days. I spent most of that time in her room watching William reliving his grief over losing me. William was in high school, and he didn't have the time or, in his adolescence, the inclination to spend more than an hour or two with my mother each day in her room as she died over the course of a week. It was William's first year driving, and he used my mother's car to go back and forth to the hospital. He never once spent the night. I didn't blame him. That week William seemed to visibly age, any remaining innocence gone. At the same time, he looked so young in the role of a grieving child. The night my mother died, I watched her from above, her grotesquely raised eyebrows and gaping mouth saying more than words ever could have. As she passed, there was no moment of us meeting in the hereafter. One minute she was there, and the next she was gone. William was on his own. Mostly. Of course, he still had me.

At that point, I started keeping closer tabs on his whereabouts and well-being. And I didn't try to hide. I let him see me as often as I thought he could handle. I believed it would help. Maybe it only helped me. At first, I followed him very closely, trying everything I could to make sure he was taken care of—though there wasn't much I could do in my condition. I occasionally found myself able to soothe him to sleep some nights. And I gave him ideas for his drawings. My artistic life was something I could still offer, and this kept us close, closer than he knew.

Back when I was a young mother, I had no friends to speak of. And no one from the hospital invited me to their barbecues or Christmas parties. A single mother would get few invitations in any case, I told myself, but I knew it was more than that. I was considered eccentric. That word hung over me like a diagnosis. But not everything I did was eccentric. I ate scrambled eggs, drank milk, baked chocolate-chip cookies, did laundry, paid my bills on time. Surely these were not the machinations of an eccentric. And it's not like I had worn a sequined nurse's uniform or read my patient's charts with a monocle. I did my job.

I did do things like meditate standing up at my desk, do my crossword puzzles out loud, and so on. But I think it was the amount of time—the inordinate amount of time—that I spent with the recently dead that gave everyone at the hospital pause. And it didn't help that I was an artist. In an attempt to keep people interested, but not too interested, I hung a few of my small paintings at work, just landscapes. Nothing far-out. But proving I was a real artist didn't help much. Still, at home, I believe it gave me many more years of near-sanity than I would have had otherwise. Painting kept me alive long enough to get to know my son and to pass something on to him other than a collection of questionable chromosomes and a life of grief. It amazes me that there are people who actually wonder what art is even for. How can a person not understand that art gives us a place to exist when there's nowhere left to go?

My studio was in the basement of our house, initially a spare bedroom. It didn't have the best light, but I made it work. Our house wasn't big enough to store the dozens of paintings I created each year for over a decade. These I kept at my mother's house and in a storage space. That's how they managed to outlive me.

When William was in art school, I would spend hours a day looking at his paintings, sometimes all day on just one section of one painting. There's more to see in a painting than there is in real life, or at least what people think of as real life. In fact, within one great painting, there are lives upon lives, a stark contrast to what's found in a single, mundane existence. The more abstract the painting, the fewer the constraints, the greater the multitudes.

Talking about painting is one thing, but losing yourself in the work is something else entirely. When William began to study painting in earnest, I often found myself wanting to try my hand again. It was so tempting to pick up where he left off. I would have loved to paint all night, to see the sun come up with a brush in my hand, like before. And I didn't even need light anymore. (Seeing in the dark is one skill, among many, that the dead have unquestionably earned.) In fact, I could stand in front of a painting—one of William's, one of mine, or one in a museum—and see it with my eyes closed. I wasn't even sure I had eyes anymore. Now, there's a conundrum—a painter who isn't even sure she has eyes? Regardless, I eventually found myself picking up my son's paints, working all night while he slept, telling myself that this was the best way I could show my love for him.

CHAPTER 7

A FEW DAYS after Pigeonhole's nosedive, I ran into Tanya in the hallway. She told me he would be at Hennepin County Medical Center for several weeks, at least, and then probably a rehab center. He had a fractured hip, three cracked ribs, a dislocated shoulder, and a spinal injury, the extent of which was unclear. But he had not suffered any brain trauma. Tanya expressed gratitude for his having escaped death, but—in a way I couldn't fully comprehend—she also seemed grateful for the incident itself. My part in it—which she was there for but didn't really witness—went unmentioned, which I appreciated.

"He's going to be okay," she eventually said in a convincing if shaky voice.

"I hope so." I sounded less convincing, but at least I said it.

Tanya cleaned the bathroom that day, removing all of Pigeonhole's dirty towels, the jar of jelly, the bowie knife, everything. Everything except the cardboard Eddie, which I moved to the closet of my apartment. From then on, the St. Jude was pleasantly quiet. The building's peaceful charm, such as it was, had returned. It was a welcome reprieve, but I knew it would never last.

My exhibition was scheduled to open in two weeks, and I wasn't anywhere close to ready. Caroline, the owner of Perimeter Gallery, had given me the show based on just a few paintings and the strong recommendation of my former professor, Vernon Nilsson. She never asked to see my progress, and I never once mentioned my lack of it. And I certainly didn't mention that I would need my mother's help if I was going to produce enough decent work to pull off this show.

Vernon, nearly seventy years old and never married, lived alone on the third floor of my building, renting nearly the entire floor as both his studio and living space. He kept his apartment windows covered in rice paper, allowing only highly diffuse light to enter during the day and never allowing the interior of his studio to be seen from the street at night. His name was synonymous with the St. Jude, or at least it was for most of the nearly thirty years he had lived there.

Vernon's artwork would occupy the cavernous main gallery space—some 2,000 square feet—and mine the smaller adjunct gallery, a room 10 by 18 feet, with lower ceilings and two small, mismatched windows stabbed into the far wall. Taking a backseat to an established and well-respected artist, one very much my senior, was all part of the game. Still, this was by far my biggest show, and I was grateful for the opportunity. Vernon had introduced me to Caroline after taking a liking to my work when I was his student at the Minneapolis College of Art and Design. He had also been the one to suggest I move into the St. Jude. At the time, I suspected he secretly owned the building. He treated it as if he did, keeping things in the building's basement, on the roof, and occupying several parking spaces with a van and three motorcycles. Vernon tinkered with the motorcycles often enough, but rarely rode them. At his age, that was probably wise. He was stout, with a head of curly white hair and a full, burly beard. This look suited him; he bore no signs of impending dissolution of health and no ill will toward the young. He had a ferocious look in his eye that was more rebellious than aggressive. A simple glance from Vernon could come off as a glare, and he could knock you over with an icy scowl. He often reeked of gin, sometimes whiskey, occasionally vodka, but most often of red wine—burgundy and cabernet were his favorites—and he kept all the corks, thousands of them, in bins on the roof of the building. On Sunday mornings, sober as a schoolboy, he'd go up on the roof and playfully toss the corks at passing cars. He had a few pigeons trained to fetch them.

Vernon made a fair amount of money both as an art professor and in the art market. But he spent it sparingly and at times strangely. He reveled in the squalor of the St. Jude and the neighborhood surrounding it. And he had enjoyed a colorful past, which he loved to share at length and at any opportunity. One of the first things he ever told me, both as an example of his past and of his desire to enumerate it in the present, was about his supposed abduction by aliens. According to Vernon, after his first abduction in 1985, he had been given a complete psychiatric evaluation by a prominent physician—a national leader in psychiatry—at the Mayo Clinic. He received a clean bill of health, with the caveat that he consider the possibility that he had hallucinated after ingesting psychedelic mushrooms. Still, a polygraph test had apparently confirmed this alien abduction story. (He had a printout of this test, which he showed me—just a bunch of squiggly lines.) Naturally, I was skeptical of all of Vernon's stories, but I didn't want to ruin my shot at showing my artwork at the best gallery in Minneapolis. I listened intently, often for hours at a time, to his quiver of questionable tales.

With so little time before my show, I was entering panic mode. I had dozens of sketches and plenty of half-baked ideas, but I was left staring at far more blank canvas than I had ever filled in such a short time. To complete the work, I had no choice but to paint twelve hours a day for two weeks straight. I stopped texting Sara and didn't hear from her for the entire two weeks. I wasn't sure if this period of silence was my doing or hers, but she knew I had to complete the work for the show, so I told myself to assume the best. But in fact, I assumed nothing at all, which I decided was even better.

Though I planned to work as hard as I could, I knew my innate abilities weren't going to be enough. I would need my mother's help. And it came. I never saw her, directly, during that two-week stretch, but each time I took a break from working on a painting, it improved. As I slept, the work advanced. Whenever I cleaned a brush, I found another covered in paint. My palette changed whenever I dared to step away. Once, while I was out walking for an hour, a painting I had barely begun was nearly complete when I returned. I had often worried I would never become the painter my mother was. With her help, I was becoming the painter I believe she wanted me to be.

Was this all in my imagination? Had it been that way my entire life? It wasn't a question I really wanted answered. In fact, it wasn't a question I truly asked myself. I accepted what I saw, disturbing, surprising, and scary as it was. I had been seeing my mother for many years, but she had never taken this kind of action before, never interfered with my materials, my ideas, or my way of working. I had no words for this, but the feeling I had was that of being a minor character in a play or a movie or a book, someone neither acting nor being acted upon, but instead someone being manipulated by another being, a creator of some sort. What do characters think and feel when they aren't the focus of their creator's attention? That's how I felt, sidelined as my mother took over my artwork and went places with it that I never could have imagined.

At the end of those two grueling weeks, I had lost ten pounds, gained a beard, and become accustomed to sleeping in my coveralls. My sheets were stained with pigment and smelled of linseed oil and turpentine. To avoid distractions, I kept the blinds closed day and night. I had lost track of time to the point of not knowing the day of the week, let alone the time of day. The fast-drying alkyd paint I used allowed me to work right up until the last day. On the final evening before I had to deliver all the work, with every painting finished except one—exhausted and disoriented, an eroded version of myself—I gave up and crashed into bed just before midnight.

When I awoke the next morning, the final painting was finished—a small, ethereal interior scene depicting a 1970s suburban kitchen, done in crayon-pure colors. It was, for all practical purposes, just a sketch the night before. But now it was refined and elegant and polished. The sight of it set off a wave of guilt; the debt to my mother was beyond measure. Still, what she did could never be set right, no matter how much help I received from her now. So why did I feel like the guilty one?

I sat at the edge of my bed and stared at that painting for twenty minutes. I asked myself how she had come up with the color scheme. The pigments didn't look like anything I had in my supplies. The hues were so vibrant, and their combinations so radical, I wondered if Caroline would question the work. It didn't have a strong connection to the other pieces, mostly desolate, dreary, or decaying suburban landscapes—tract houses, sunbaked lawns, new construction bumping up against farmland, all of it painted in much more subdued colors, expressing an entirely different constellation of emotions. This one had the least input from me, but it seemed like it was the best of the lot. Maybe it represented a new direction, signified a new body of work, something on the horizon. Some untapped potential. Whatever it was, I hoped it was something Caroline could sink her teeth into, and, more importantly, sell to her collectors. I signed the painting in the lower righthand corner and set to work packing everything up.

I managed to fit all the paintings into the back of my old Volvo station wagon. Just before noon I left my apartment with only a skeletal sense of myself, but that skeleton wore a garment of satisfaction. With one painting blocking the rear window and one painting poking me in the ribs, I drove downtown.

Caroline's gallery was in the Minneapolis North Loop where, twenty-five years earlier, there had been a spirited assortment of artists, galleries, and patrons, all of whom braved the raw winter winds and the humid, heavy summer nights to support local artists. Back then there were several dozen viable galleries. But now, Perimeter Gallery was wedged between two sports bars across the street from a new police station. Any signs of the old guard were few and far between. Caroline somehow made it work. She owned the building (meaning her rent never went up), and she leaned on her well-established connection to a certain cross section of the Minneapolis elite, a few important people who bought just enough artwork to keep things afloat. These collectors didn't necessarily buy a lot of art compared to their East and West Coast counterparts, but they needed to make sure there was one place where they could. That place was Perimeter Gallery.

I found Caroline sitting behind her desk, eating Lay's potato chips and drinking a Diet Coke. She looked to be on approximately page 1333 of the novel 2666. She didn't glance up until I cleared my throat. Caroline was thin, some might say too thin, with spiky, naturally blond hair, a prominent collarbone, and a knife-edge jawline.

"William." She put the book down. "You look refreshed. Is Pigeonhole out on tour or something?"

"Didn't I tell you? He's in the hospital. He fell down the stairs and broke a bunch of stuff. He won't be touring for a while, I don't think."

"Wow. Bad heroin will get you every time." She pointed at me. "Remember I said that. Now, let me see ... where were we on having that show of your mother's paintings?"

"The same place we were before. Nowhere."

Caroline was willful, occasionally wild-eyed, criminally opportunistic, but always with a detective's incredulousness. "You should never have shown me any of her paintings. It's the best body of unknown work I've ever seen. If you sell half of them and hold onto the other half, you'll never have to work again."

"I don't want to never work again."

I went back to my car. One by one I pulled my paintings out. Every one of them looked awful to me, especially those on which I received the least help from my mother. I felt like a feeble, poorly trained assistant compared to her, or to Vernon, or to anyone. There was no way I could have pulled this show together without my mother's help. This really was a show of her work, in a way. Swallowing the thought, I kept moving the paintings, one or two at a time, into the gallery.

The space was smaller than I had remembered, and I began to wonder if such a cramped show was a good idea. The walls were bright white—too white—but Caroline wouldn't let me paint them a more subdued shade. "Rules are rules," she said. "And I make the rules." It took me a few hours to hang the show. I received no help or direction. In fact, Caroline left to run an errand.

While she was gone, Vernon arrived in a rented moving van with two hired hands who carried his work into the gallery. His show consisted of a large, rough-hewn antique dining table from Austria, large-scale photographs, several dozen vials of dry blood and assorted chemicals, and hundreds of long white strands of hair, which I assumed were his own. On the table, he had carved the word *synecdoche*. His artist statement, affixed to the wall near the gallery entrance, defined the word:

> "Synecdoche" is a kind of metonymy in which the whole is substituted for a part, a part for the whole, the general for the specific, or the specific for the general, as in "blade" for "knife," or "John Hancock" for "signature."

He also had a dozen close-up photographs of more hair, fingernails, fluids of some sort, vials, plastic bags, buttons, money, confetti, and other detritus. The photographs were gorgeous in color, expertly printed, beautifully framed, limited edition, and very expensive. None of it made any sense whatsoever.

Vernon walked into the adjunct gallery. He glanced at a few of my paintings. "Your work looks good, William," he said, facing me and pointing, for some reason, at his own head. "The curators from the Walker will be at the closing reception, so you should be ready to answer a few questions. But that won't be for six weeks, so you have some time to prepare." Caroline had closing receptions instead of opening receptions so she could end the show in a buying frenzy. It seemed to work for her. "And now that you have finished this body of work, you can paint that life-sized portrait of your mother you've talked about."

None of your business; not your concern, I thought. But I didn't want to challenge his artistic wisdom here, now, in the gallery, in front of my work, and his work, and his assistants, and him. "I suppose I could try," I responded.

"I'll knock on the floor once in a while to give you a gentle reminder. But I won't be around for a bit. I leave for Tau Ceti B tomorrow morning."

Vernon's obsession with outer space was no secret. On the roof of the St. Jude were more than a dozen homemade satellite dishes that he used to listen for signals from various constellations. His devotion to this enterprise even caught the attention of the Department of Homeland Security.

"Do you want me to water your plants while you're up there?" I asked.

"Good one," he said. "Kidding, of course. I'm just going to Duluth to relax for a few days." He put his hand on my shoulder. "Take care, now. I have a good feeling about this show."

Vernon left with his assistants. Caroline returned a few minutes later. She was overwhelmed by the gallery's transformation as she took in Vernon's work. After more than a minute of silence, she said, "Is he done?"

"I guess so," I said.

"Wow." Caroline was doing her "I'm so lucky to be alive" gape, which really meant she might get a write-up in *Hyperallergic*. She began to rub her hand along the surface of Vernon's table, feeling the carved wood with agile fingers. She reluctantly pulled her hand away and said, "We need to get the light right. Bad lighting will kill this show." She looked over into the adjunct gallery. "Can you do me a favor, William?" She pointed at a painting I had decided, at the last minute, to hang between the two windows. "Take that one home. It doesn't fit it with the rest."

It was the only one my mother hadn't helped me with. I took it down and brought it out to my car. I tossed the painting in the dumpster when I got home.

CHAPTER 8

WHEN YOU ARE bound up inside yourself (for example, after spending two straight weeks doing little else than listening to your own thoughts and recording the physical responses to those thoughts in paint on canvas), you might discover that life isn't—and can never be—just coil. There must be re-coil. To put it more succinctly, I needed to unwind. But I wasn't ready to stray too far from home, so I headed down-stairs to the TimeWarp.

I sent Sara a one-word text: "Finished." She didn't re-spond right away. Sara and I hadn't seen each other, talked on the phone, or even texted since the night of the explosion, and—looking back on it all now—I'd say rightly so. She had been appalled by my reaction to Pigeonhole's jump, but more so by my self-isolation and obsessive devotion to my artwork for those two weeks. It wasn't normal. Not even close. But at the time, I didn't see it that way. It was simply necessary.

As I entered the bar, I received a one-word response from Sara: "TimeWarp?"

I texted back: "Already there."

Sara arrived just before I finished my first beer. She sat down next to me and signaled the bartender. The smell of popcorn, popped carelessly—too hot and in too much oil—wafted its way through the bar. Sara's face reflected the cobalt blue bar light, and her heavy perfume overpowered the rancid stench in the air. She pulled off her coat, revealing a trim top that was months out of season. That wasn't unusual for her. But with an early spring snow in the forecast and the temperature dropping, she at least had enough sense to wear a wool hat, a knit scarf, and leggings—all of it black, as usual. I was still in my painting coveralls, though I had not painted anything that day, and didn't plan to for some time. I needed to recover. But I wondered if my mother was upstairs already at work on another painting.

Sara didn't have much to say at first, but maybe that was my fault. I was talking quickly, moving from topic to topic, as if my thoughts were somehow months out of season as well. When I began to describe Vernon's artwork at length, Sara's face told me she wasn't there to listen to me ramble. She was there to say something specific. So of course I kept going on and on. I told her about my show, how the paintings looked, what Caroline thought, and what I'd be doing now that the work was complete. She let me talk. She remarked on the weight I'd lost and seemed genuinely concerned. But she held back what she intended to say until it was too late to say it.

We went upstairs. In my dark apartment—too dark to see Sara's face just a foot away from mine on the pillow beside me—she said, "Why didn't you text or call this entire time?"

"I had to work"

"The entire time?"

"I couldn't handle any distractions."

"So you're saying I'm a distraction?"

"That's not what I meant."

"Yes, it was." Sara held back for a moment, but I knew what was coming. She drew a deep breath and said, "William, I don't think I can do this anymore."

She sat up on the bed next to me and looked up at the ceiling. This was something she had done a hundred times before, but this time it felt different. It felt as if she were taking a final look around. Although I was somewhat prepared to hear this, I had been wishing it away, hoping she would chicken out or have a last-minute change of heart. No such luck. I was glad I had done all that talking, all that stalling, because if I had heard this any earlier in the evening, especially if I had heard it at the bar, I might have broken down crying. I had never cried in front of Sara, and I didn't want it to happen that way.

We sat together in silence. It wasn't lost on me that with Pigeonhole gone I had experienced two full weeks of near silence, day and night. I had wanted to comment on it, about how much peace there had been in the building, but I didn't want to bring the still-raw memory of the incident back to the present moment.

"Did you hear me?" she asked.

Of course I had heard her, but I remained silent. She was breaking up with me, and I didn't have the wherewithal to respond. There was no response, other than acceptance, that would have made any sense. The act of breaking up with me was the only sensible choice. I had been relying on the fact that Sara had not been sensible up to this point. If there was room for doubt, it was where the tipping point had come. Was it Pigeonhole's jump and my part in it? Was it not calling or texting her for two weeks? Was there someone else? Maybe it was a combination of things. I had a feeling she was about to tell me.

"Well, if you're not going to talk, I will. We don't have normal conversations anymore anyway. Or even dysfunctional conversations. There's something deeper going on. You're so distracted all the time. Half the time I feel like there's someone else in the room with us."

She couldn't have known, of course, but that was so utterly perceptive of her it scared the shit out of me.

"Like who?" I asked. "Literally who else would be in the room with us?"

"I don't mean someone literally in the room."

I did mean someone literally in the room, but I wasn't going to elaborate.

"Can you just tell me if anything I'm saying makes sense to you?" she asked, sounding like someone trying to get directions from a statue they've mistaken for a real person.

"Of course it makes sense. I'm distracted beyond all reason. I do, in fact, act like there's someone else in the room half the time. Something deeper is definitely going on. But in my defense, none of this is anything new."

Sara was silent. Perhaps she wasn't expecting me to agree so completely. She certainly wasn't wrong. Then again, neither was I.

"This is maybe the first time I actually miss Pigeonhole," I said. "I wish he were here now, playing so fucking loud that we couldn't have this conversation." I shocked myself that I had thought such a thing, let alone said it out loud, but it was the truth. Pigeonhole had been the perfect distraction.

"I hope he's going to be okay," she said.

I hadn't meant to start a conversation on the topic, but at least it diverted us, if only briefly, from the breakup.

"Down at the TimeWarp," I said, "word is he's still in pretty rough shape. But no serious head injury, apparently. Mostly broken bones. And something in his spine."

"His spine?" Sara gasped. "Is it permanent?"

"I'm not sure. He can move his legs somewhat, but he can't walk, at least not yet. There's a long road ahead."

"Has Tanya been around?"

"I heard someone shuffling around in there the other day, so I knocked, and it was her. Pigeonhole wanted her to pick up some of his stuff. She hasn't been back since. I don't imagine she's too keen on hanging out here by herself."

"I feel sorry for her," Sara said. "She's so nice. I mean, nicer than you'd think, from looking at her. Too nice for Harry, anyway."

"She is too nice for him," I agreed. "The only time I ever heard her raise her voice was when he asked her not to sing. He wanted her to just play along with the tambourine. She got really upset and started yelling, 'Don't pigeonhole me!' over and over. That's how he got the idea for his stage name."

"Really? You never told me that."

"It happened right when I moved in. Before I met you. I kind of forgot about it."

"William, I'm sorry."

"Sorry?"

"I didn't mean to get off track. I came with something to say, and I need to say it now. There's a wall between us that I should have acknowledged was always there. And I don't think you want the wall to come down. I need a break from trying to get over that wall."

I didn't want to agree with her, but she was right. The wall was there, and I didn't have the skills, or the time, or even much desire, to try to knock it down. The wall kept me safe, safe from the kind of loss I always felt was inevitable anyway, the kind of loss that would be easier to deal with from a distance.

"If you're breaking up with me," I said, "it should be more dramatic."

"Dramatic? Jesus, William, can we have a conversation without having a conversation about the conversation?"

"I'm just saying."

"And I'm just saying the world has enough drama." Sara stood up and stepped into her boots. "Not to mention the drama inside your head."

I leaned over to my nightstand, picked up a box of matches, and lit a candle. I stared at the flame as Sara put on her hat and scarf.

"At the very least, I need a break," she said. "I'll call you."

I could faintly hear the wick sizzle. I wished desperately for something clever to say, something so clever she would reverse course right there, undress, and climb back into bed with me. I wanted nothing more in that moment. But no words came. Sara let herself out. When I heard the door of the building slam shut, I blew out the candle and let the silence and darkness take over.

If I had been honest with myself, I'd have admitted I got what I deserved. But the truth is I was too distracted to think properly. Too distracted by my paintings, by my mother's presence, by my own thoughts, and by my own desires. I may have wanted to acknowledge my own failures, but at the time I didn't know how. Instead, all I wanted was a second chance.

Chapter 9

My mother had blue-gray eyes, dark brown hair, and very pale skin, even in the summertime. She was short, about five-one. She carried herself gracefully, often wore high heels, whether out on the town or at home. She never left the house without makeup, or failed to curl her hair or her long eyelashes. At age five or six, I began to consciously admire her beauty. I felt lucky to be near her. But, because we rarely embraced, there was a kind of detachment to the admiration. More often than not, she was distant, cold. Every once in a while, though, she would pull me toward her, caress my head gently, and tell me that she loved me.

Much of her energy was spent keeping her mental health in check. In the best of times, she was successful. At her worst, she would fall apart at the seams. Her final diagnosis was schizophrenia. Even with that diagnosis, which I knew little about at the time, I got the feeling she thought she was possessed. That, or she was being controlled by extraterrestrials, or by the government, or both. As a kid, I found all of this (up to a certain point) to be pretty amusing. And, because no doctor or other authority figure had stepped in to suggest otherwise, I felt safe. I had always held out hope that she was merely playing an elaborate gag on everyone around her, a gag she assumed I knew was just that. The idea that I was in on the gag—though we could never acknowledge it—was a solace. By the time she got really sick, she had lost a lot of weight and much of her verve. But her gaunt face became that much more angelic to me, her lips fuller in contrast to the hard-edged countenance they adorned. Soon, her teeth began to yellow. Her eyes turned a gray the color of cigarette smoke. She quit gardening and rarely went outside. Toward the end she built a pyramid-shaped meditation chamber in our basement. That was the place they found her body.

Before I was born, my mother worked as a registered nurse. In her grade school years, she'd been an A student, earning a scholarship to Hamline University in St. Paul and taking full advantage of her high IQ. Her superior intelligence did not serve her well once she began working at St. Joseph's, the hospital where I would eventually be delivered. I often wondered if I was also conceived there, since my mother so rarely allowed men in our house. She always specified women plumbers, carpenters, meter-readers, and electricians. Her requests were usually met. The tone of her voice or the look on her face was all the explanation needed.

While in nursing school, she could, off the top of her head, recall rare drug interactions that seasoned physicians were expected to look up in manuals. She would correct the interns' mistakes before they knew they had made them. And she knew all the union agreements. No male doctor dared let his words stray or his eyes linger, refer to her as anything but Nurse Link, or recommend she go home and get her beauty sleep the way they too often did with the other female nurses. She told me all of this many times when I was too young to really understand what it all meant. She quit that hospital the day she went into labor with me and didn't return to work there again.

She waited years before she came back to me. But I did feel her presence in some sense, even on the day she died. And I suspected that she was the one moving my art supplies, scratching notes in my books, flipping my albums over on the turntable. But I didn't start to actually see her until I set up an easel in my grandmother's basement for the first time. When I became frustrated with my initial attempt at a simple landscape, my mother appeared in the corner of the room. I remember she laughed, but I couldn't hear her. It seemed she couldn't hear me, either. Or maybe she just ignored me when I asked if it was really her. Although I was shocked to see her, I wasn't scared. Not at first. But of course I was scared that I might be losing my mind, just like her. After a few minutes, she started to fade in and out, and no longer seemed to be aware that I was there. As I approached her, she disappeared completely. From then on, she appeared to me once every few weeks on average, and only for minutes or sometimes just seconds at a time.

Besides being a nurse, she had the beginnings of a career as a successful artist. She died right before a big show that she'd landed in New York. They held the show posthumously, and, possibly as a result of her suicide, the show was a modest success. Through my mother's estate, I ended up with a bit of money from the show, something like $10,000, but it didn't last. Neither did her notoriety. Most of her paintings were in storage and survived the fire. The bulk of them were later moved to a storage locker my grandmother rented out in the far suburbs. She paid the storage fee for years ahead. Over the years, I cobbled together enough money to keep the work there.

Her paintings had craggy and varnished surfaces that were glinty and beautiful. As a teenager, I kept one of her abstract pieces in my bedroom. It had green and umber vermiculation underneath gold and carmine peaks moving like radio waves across a background as black as outer space. It felt cosmic and timeless, yet intimate and fleeting. How my mother conveyed all this in one abstract work of art I may never know. It was as if she could hear the paint as it dried, as if she could tune the canvas like a vibrating drum. Her bigger pieces were symphonic, the smaller ones like melodies suited perfectly to the space they occupied. There was so much movement in her work that the walls where they hung seemed to sway and hum. She did all this with the tools a painter is limited to: pigment and oil, a brush, palette knives, her fingers—but how? There are things in her work I could never hope to accomplish. At least not without her help.

When she was alive, my mother read to me late into the evening practically every night; she sat right next to me as I slept, a glass of wine on the table beside her, a bottle of pills tucked under the chair cushions. She read mostly contemporary literature, novels and stories. As I'd drift off, she'd continue to read until one or two in the morning in the chair next to my bed. I loved her presence in my room, a living, breathing, thinking presence that never really left me.

CHAPTER 10

I SPENT THE following week organizing my art supplies, eating, hydrating, doing everything I could to recover from the marathon of the previous weeks. I managed to gain a couple of pounds, get back into the routine of shaving and showering, and even found time for some mild exercise, jogging along the Mississippi for a few miles here and there. But emotionally I hadn't recovered. I felt stuck, dead inside. I hadn't seen my mother that week, which was not unusual, but it felt like an eternity. For my entire adult life and much of my adolescence, I had seen her every few days, or at least seen evidence of her presence in moved objects, finished paintings, a made bed, or music left playing on my stereo. There was none of that for the entire week.

Friday came, and I remembered that Sara had planned a party for that night—she had told me about it weeks earlier—and, although she did not explicitly uninvite me, I was sure she would be unhappy to see me. So, of course, I decided to get drunk and crash it.

Sara's apartment was just across the river from mine, an easy ten-minute walk, even when intoxicated. At around nine-thirty, I took a final shot of Jim Beam and tripped down the stairs into the surprisingly warm April air. I crossed the

10th Avenue bridge and followed the undulating sidewalk to her ground-floor apartment near the east bank. From the sidewalk outside, I could hear live bluegrass music—amateurish but earnest—pouring from the windows, which made me shiver. The idea of Sara having anything to do with bluegrass musicians was so out of character I worried that she had fallen into the clutches of a cult of some sort.

The door to her building was propped open. This was a relief because it meant I didn't have to use my key, nor would I have to return it. I went upstairs. Upon entering the party, I counted three acoustic guitars, a banjo, two violins, and a musical saw all being hacked on by Sara's guests. I had never seen any of these people before. In fact, I had never heard live bluegrass before. Were these her friends? I steadied myself against the music and went into the kitchen where I found Stan Einstein trying to get beer from an obviously empty keg. I knew him from his music store; he was a bit of a local legend in the Minneapolis music scene. Tall and thin with paper-white skin, he had a reddish nose and a shock of blond hair that matched his last name well enough. He wore a grungy wool sweater, thick tortoise-shell glasses, and jeans so skinny he looked like a schoolboy who had outgrown his only pair of pants. At the keg, he pumped and pumped but got only a few fizzles of beer.

He looked over at me. "Bill, right?"

"Have we met?" I asked. He seemed to be looking at my mouth. Was there something stuck in my teeth?

"Sara showed me a photo." He smiled and kept pumping the tap. "I was just telling Sara that after tonight I'm kind of laying off beer for a while. I think I use it too much. Like, I don't drink it, I use it. Know what I mean?"

I did. His music store, Emcee Squared, was a hybrid of guitars, guitar amplifiers, and a carefully curated selection of vinyl records. His taste was well regarded around town, but the store came across as pretentious to me. Not that the selection was so terrible. However, as an imbecile would deliver the mail (colored envelopes in one mailbox, white in another, coupons and shopping guides in another, and so forth), so Einstein organized his records: super groups of the seventies in one section (ABBA, Fleetwood Mac, the Eagles), mono recordings in another (Robert Johnson, Grateful Dead bootlegs, stand-up comedy), Canadian artists in another (Joni Mitchell, Neil Diamond, Gordon Lightfoot), and so on. He got away with it by claiming it was the only way he could remember where everything was.

"Like when I don't know what else to do," he continued without prompting, "I just drink beer. As in, shit, I slammed my finger in my car door, which I did yesterday, so I drank a beer. Or, shit, I forgot to feed the fish, might as well have another beer. Can't give beer to the fish, though, right? Or wait, can I? Anyway, the other day I was like, sweet, I got an A-minus on my paper on Sid Vicious—which I did; I'm taking classes at Macalester—so I guess I'll have a beer. By the way, it's a night class, but they count for credit. Anyway, I think if I use beer less, I could get a straight A on my next paper, which, as it happens, is on Richard Hell."

The tap sputtered again, and he continued pumping. I left the kitchen and found Sara out on her back porch, alone. She was sitting in a beanbag chair flipping through Instagram. She looked so beautiful in the glow of her phone that I wanted to weep, but I stuffed the feeling and cleared my throat.

"Shouldn't you be entertaining your guests?" I asked. "Or helping Einstein with the keg?"

"Christ." Sara was startled. "What are you doing here? You should be at home sulking."

"What I do is not sulking. It's waiting."

She stood and put her phone in her back pocket. "And what exactly are you waiting for?"

"That's what I'm waiting to find out," I said. Telling her that I was, in fact, waiting for my mother to walk through the wall at any moment wasn't the reason I had crashed her party. But I was struggling to think of the exact reason I had crashed her party. Just making my presence known wasn't enough.

"As long as you're here, can you give my keys back? I can go find yours."

"I didn't bring them," I lied. "And you can keep mine for now."

"It will just take a minute."

"No really, keep them. You never know."

"Okay, but let's agree that we'll be exchanging keys at some point."

"Okay, let's."

"Yes, let's." She tried to say that as casually as possible. "So why are you here?"

"I see Stan is enjoying himself. Are these his people?"

"They're not his people. I mean, they are his friends, yes. He's starting a new band. Kind of an alt-country thing."

"More like bluegrass?"

"Okay, sure, you could call it that."

I rolled my eyes. "Did you see that? I just rolled my eyes."

"It's dark in here, but I believe you."

Sara's phone rang. It was her father, she said. She excused herself and went down the hallway to her bedroom.

I backtracked through the kitchen, past Einstein who was still pumping the keg, to the living room. As I tiptoed through the music-makers, someone tapped me on the shoulder. It was Clarissa.

"I'm surprised to see you here," she said.

"I'm surprised to see you here," I said.

"Why?"

"The bluegrass," I replied. "I can't imagine you wanting to hear the sound of a live banjo."

"It grows on you," she said. "If you let it. By the way, I saw you talking with Stan."

"I'm really not sure what Sara sees in him."

"Aside from the fact that he isn't you?" Clarissa was holding two full glasses of white wine and handed me one. I immediately downed half of it.

"At least there's that," I said.

She laughed, leaned toward me, and whispered: "By the way, here's something to know about Stan. Ready for this? He wears a hairpiece. Nothing too extreme, but what you see is not all his." She seemed delighted to be giving me this information.

I gulped down the rest of the wine and scanned the room. Stan had given up on the keg and picked up a guitar. Unprompted, he began to sing a sloppy rendition of "Teddy Bear," which everyone thought was great, but which, in fact, was ghastly by any reasonable measure. He made quick work of it, at least. There was applause, and even a whistle. Sara entered the room. Clarissa had the wine bottle in her hand and refilled my glass. Einstein started playing one of his own songs, a painful ditty that had been a local quasi-hit about ten years before. He'd written and recorded it while lead singer of an emo band called the Moodscreamers:

> Vintage clothes wearer
> I think we should do it
> In your apartment
> Or while driving to it.
>
> I shouldn't have said that
> I guess I just blew it

But vintage clothes wearer
Your dress made me do it.

I was repulsed. What did people see in this person? Beyond that, why did he even exist? Why was I here? Why did I exist? I was slipping fast.

"I'm leaving," I said to Clarissa. "I can't take any more of this."

"Not yet," she said, keeping her voice quiet. "We need to talk."

Just then someone handed Einstein a banjo, an instrument that he, in fact, did not play, and he began to perform Pete Townshend-style windmills on it. It was sacrilegious, both to actual banjoists and The Who, but also stupid. At that moment, I vowed to never crash another party again as long as I lived. Since I was never invited to parties, that meant no more parties for me again, ever.

"This is giving me a migraine," I said. "I shouldn't have come here." I handed Clarissa the glass.

"Let's go to the bar," she suggested. "Your bar. The Time-Warp. You and me right now. That might get Sara's attention."

"Attention? What does that mean? I don't want Sara's attention."

"Then what are you doing here?"

"Okay, fine," I conceded. "But what's in it for you?"

"Consider it a favor. Then someday, I can ask for one in return."

"Sounds like an offer I can't refuse."

Clarissa ditched the wine, and we made our way toward the door. We walked across the river to the TimeWarp mostly in silence. The sounds of banjo strings, tambourine jangles, and a jaw harp bounced around in my head.

"Was that actually a 'jug band'?" I asked. "Isn't that what you call a bad bluegrass band?"

"I think so. Stan is really embracing his Americana phase."

"Please tell me it's only a phase."

"I guess he has a record deal again. Just a local label, but still. The embrace is total, at least for now."

I had no response to this, so I focused on what I was going to order when we got to the bar.

"Why is this place called the TimeWarp?" Clarissa asked when we arrived.

"A time warp is a hypothetical distortion of time in which events at different moments can be brought together or experienced out of their normal sequence as if time itself were bent," I said. "So says Wikipedia. It's also on the menu, which I've read a million times."

"Okay, but what does that have to do with a dive bar?"

"It's supposed to funnel you away from all your troubles, I think. Bring you to a happier time and place as quickly as possible."

"Isn't every bar in town trying to do that?" She looked at me as if I'd literally been to every bar in town.

"At least this one isn't pretending to be something it's not," I said.

We sat at my usual table in the back corner. I needed to decompress, and Clarissa seemed to realize this.

"I'll go get us some drinks," she said. "What are you having?"

"Whatever you're having."

I sat alone for a moment, distracted as I so often was by the possibility of my mother dropping through the ceiling or floating into the bar through the kitchen or materializing right in front of me.

Clarissa returned with two cans of Fosters and sat down opposite from me. She popped them both open, sliding one across the table.

"Cheers," she said with no hint of sarcasm.

"Cheers, I guess."

She took a big swig, then stared at me until I did the same.

"Have you talked to Sara about us?" I asked point-blank. "I mean, about our breakup?"

"Of course," she said.

"I mean, what did you talk about?"

"What is it you're asking?"

It didn't seem worth it to beat around the bush. "I'm asking if it's really over. Like 100 percent never-going-back-to-him over. Like over over."

"I don't know about over over, but definitely over for now. But I'm pretty sure it will be over over if you crash another one of her parties."

"So why Einstein, of all people?"

"Well, they have a history. The Moodscreamers was her favorite band back in the day."

"Yuck."

"He's not so bad, you know."

I took this to mean she thought I, by contrast, was so bad.

"His music store is fun, and his online sales are really good. He's making money and knows the business inside out."

"So?" I was plowing through the Fosters.

"So he's not struggling. I guess it's one less thing to worry about."

"Meaning my shitty career choice isn't working for her?"

"She loves your artwork. She thinks you're a genius. So does my father, for what it's worth."

"I can't help it if my paintings don't make money."

"There's more to it than that."

"Such as?"

"Such as the way you won't ever sleep at Sara's in case you have to get up and paint in the middle of the night."

"I have no choice. That's just how it works."

"It's not only that stuff," Clarissa said. "It's everything."

"Everything?"

"Yeah, everything. In any case, it's not really for me to say. Sara is Sara. She wants what she wants and doesn't want what she doesn't want. You know that by now."

I was listening, but looking across the bar, wondering if I'd see my mother. But there were only the usual patrons. A few passersby on the street outside. No one else.

"What is it?" Clarissa asked. She turned around.

"Nothing. I just get distracted sometimes."

She turned back. "There's your answer right there," she said. "All I can suggest for now is to be patient. If Sara gets bored with Stan, or frustrated, or pissed, she'll make it known."

We sat for a few minutes in silence. I tried as hard as I could to not look around the bar. To not be distracted. It was difficult. Clarissa appeared to find this amusing. We finished our beers.

"I have to go," she said, crushing her can. "Can you walk me back to the party?"

Of course I agreed. We again crossed the river mostly in silence. Once within sight of the building, we said good night, and that was that.

CHAPTER 11

As I HEADED back across the river toward my apartment, I felt numb, unsure of anything, other than how unsure I was of everything. The night was cloudless. The ambient light of the city and a bright full moon illuminated the Mississippi below. I stopped halfway across the bridge to look at the swiftly flowing water and the flood plain beyond. The river was high from the recent snowmelt. I held my keys to Sara's apartment over the railing and considered dropping them just to watch them fall. The next thing I knew, I nearly did drop them. I had been startled by a man approaching me quickly, causing me to juggle the keys. It was Vernon, whistling the theme to *Close Encounters of the Third Kind* as he ambled up to me. He was dressed in a vintage three-piece suit stretched tightly over his large frame. He held a fedora in one hand and a suitcase in the other.

"What did you drop?" he asked, leaning over the railing.

"I didn't, but I almost did. Just some old keys." I held them up.

"Your pocket is the right place for those."

He set the suitcase down and pulled a small flashlight from his pocket. Pointing it straight down, he flashed the water intermittently in what appeared to be Morse code. He twisted the barrel of the flashlight to narrow the beam. Something buzzed, and he checked his wrist. "Five thousand steps! You know, William, all these damned devices are becoming a real burden if you ask me. I think I'll have a blintz."

He opened his suitcase and drew his finger across a cache of pastries like a henchman picking out an ax. "Care for one?"

"Why are you hauling around a suitcase full of pastries?"

"Aliens love anything filled or stuffed. That's why they gave us blintzes and Bill Gates."

"Aliens gave us Bill Gates?"

"You think a mind like that is of Earth origin?" He grabbed a blintz and snapped the suitcase shut. He pointed the flashlight at me. "Say, you look kind of down. You're not thinking of jumping, are you?"

"Not really. I mean, not tonight." I made sure to look serious, which I was. "I'm just going to go home, alone, and fire Pigeonhole's slingshot at a few cockroaches in his absence."

"Oh, I don't miss that guy. He was not in tune. Aliens hate disharmony. They like programmed music. Again, the Gates connection."

"I'm afraid I don't—"

"Afraid, yes. And it takes courage to face your fears, William. And don't you actually fear that aliens might be real? Or worse yet, that they might not be real?"

"I was going to say—"

"Courage!" He looked me in the eye. "Courage means heart, William. Heart!" Vernon pumped his fist. "The Lion wanted courage, and the Tin Man wanted a heart. Same thing!"

"What about Dorothy?" I asked.

He cocked his head. "What about her?"

"She just wanted to go home. Like me."

"Roger that," Vernon said. He picked up his suitcase. "By the way, I'm hearing good things about our show. I have a feeling Caroline will owe you some money soon."

"I hope so."

"Cross your fingers she pays you on time."

"Roger," I said, stuffing the keys into my pocket, "that."

Vernon tipped his hat and continued the opposite way across the bridge. I didn't think to ask him where he was going at this hour with a suitcase full of blintzes, but I probably wouldn't have liked the answer. I made my way home.

Thank God, I thought, my paintings are selling. I imagined paying off some of my credit cards, making a dent in my student loans, getting caught up on rent, even taking an overnight trip outside the city—things I hadn't allowed myself to imagine for years.

When I entered my apartment, I found that my old TV had turned itself on. PBS, the only digital broadcast channel that came in clearly, was airing a documentary about South Dakota. The narrator said, in a voice meant to instill awe, "Rushmore Cave, the closest cave to Mount Rushmore, is the region's largest stalactite cave." I was certain Vernon would have a theory on the veracity of that statement. I turned off the TV and unplugged it. I sat down on the bed and thought about my future, about Sara, about everything. Just then I felt an odd presence. My mother was nowhere to be seen, and whenever I felt her presence, it was nothing like this. I opened the closet. There he was, Eddie Van Halen, right where I had set him, in all his vintage cardboard glory. I pulled him out of the closet and placed him next to my easel. Maybe this was the companion I needed. A cardboard icon. Someone who never talked. Someone who continuously smiled. Someone simply there to remind me that the only thing worse than being haunted is being alone.

A cockroach crawled up the wall behind the TV. I pulled Pigeonhole's slingshot out from underneath the bed. It was a relatively high-powered model with an arm brace and long, medical-grade rubber bands. I pulled the pouch back and fired. A miss, of course, since I had nothing in the pouch. I rummaged around in my closet for a jar of marbles I had stashed away. I sat back on my bed, put a marble in the pouch, and took a shot. A bad miss. I tried a few more. The cockroach seemed unfazed and just kept marching up the wall, even after several close calls. After more than a dozen attempts, I scored a direct hit. The roach fell to the floor, stunned, but not dead. I got up and stomped it. I had heard Pigeonhole firing that slingshot at cockroaches so many times I hadn't believed it was possible to actually hit one. It was uniquely satisfying. I put the slingshot back under the bed. A moment later, there was a knock at the door.

"Who is it?"

"It's Sara, you fucking asshole."

"You have a key," I reminded her. I heard jingling, then the lock turning. She came in and staggered around the room, ripping off her clothes and throwing each garment at me. She was smashed.

"Move over," she said as she fell onto the bed.

"What are you doing here?"

"Never mind." She pointed toward Eddie. "Where did that come from?"

"Tanya left it in the bathroom. At least I think it was her. Anyhow, it was in the way, so I brought it in here."

"His smile. It's so genuine."

"Indeed, it was."

She shivered. "Why is the ceiling fan on? I'm freezing."

"It came on by itself."

"William, nothing comes on by itself. Think about it."

I thought about it as the ceiling fan rotated in what seemed to be slowly widening circles, tracing the path of a lost planet spiraling away from its mother sun. Soon Sara slipped into unconsciousness.

I kept a bottle of gin in the drawer of my nightstand. I pulled it out and took a swig, then another. What was Sara doing here? What happened with Einstein? At some point, I gave up thinking about it and drifted into sleep. That might have been the soundest night's sleep of my life. When I woke up the next morning, Sara was gone. And the key to my apartment was on the nightstand right next to the empty bottle of gin.

Chapter 12

WHEN WILLIAM WAS a toddler, I used to pick up the phone and just listen. I didn't wait for it to ring, didn't intend to call anyone. It was the dial tone I cared about. For some reason, that particular sound—350 Hz and 440 Hz together—stopped the voices in my head. When the tone ended after thirty seconds, I'd slam down the receiver and pick it up again. If I was fast enough, the voices didn't get a word in. But eventually, of course, life intervened, and I had to put the phone down. Sometimes the voices remained suppressed, at least until I had time to pick up the phone again. But more often than not, the voices began shouting all at once like spirits trapped in a genie's bottle. If I was lucky, it would just be a bunch of instructions for the day: Go shopping! Get your hair done! Teach William fractions! Take out the trash! But if I was unlucky, the voices would berate me for purposely keeping them at bay with that dial tone. After their scolding, they would give me ideas like: Lock yourself in your car in the hot sun, or, Run down the street in your high heels screaming bloody murder, or, Stick your head in the oven; see what it feels like. And, as always, defying the voices meant there would be hell to pay. They never gave up because they knew I would eventually listen.

The final time I picked up the telephone, there was no dial tone. Or at least I perceived none. Instead, there was a calm, matter-of-fact voice on the other end of the line. This is what it told me to do: Bring your precious boy to his grandmother's house, drive yourself home, and burn your house to the ground. If you do that, you'll never hear from us again. I hung up. I had always known the voices to be liars, but for some reason, this time I believed what I heard. I also knew I would do whatever it took to silence them for good.

I had spent many years trying to find the right combination of antipsychotic medications, antidepressants, and sleep aids to make life bearable. There were times when I had more or less achieved a functional equilibrium. In the years just before William was born, I would go months without hallucinating. But that all ended a few years into being a single mother. At that point, it seemed as if nothing would help. Or, to be more precise, it seemed that everything I tried ended in disaster. On the last day of my life, as the flames began to consume me, there was a moment when I thought I was gone forever, along with those many voices. That I had won. But that moment lasted for just a fraction of a second. Then I realized I was dead, but I wasn't gone.

Over time, the reason became clear enough. I was there to care for my son in ways I could not when I was alive. It wasn't easy, for either of us. For his sake, I knew it couldn't last forever, that eventually it would have to stop. For one thing, over time he grew tired of me. I could see that. I swore that once he no longer needed me, I would leave him alone. Yet I remained, convinced he did still need me. It was as if I were waiting for a voice to tell me when to wander off forever and do whatever it is dead people do when they're no longer attached to the living. But the voices were long gone.

Chapter 13

BOTH BEFORE AND after my mother's death, my school life was nondescript—just an average, Midwestern, suburban education. No one in any of my schools, whether teachers or other staff members, ever asked about my home life beyond the basics. When I said that I lived with my grandmother, most of my teachers just nodded and stared into the middle distance. Further questions ceased. Instead of me, it was as if the teachers were trying to protect themselves. I had no behavioral problems, for the most part, and I'm sure the teachers were too busy with the kids who did to bother with me.

It was my grandmother, of course, who gave me the news about my mother. She told me something terrible had happened. Something that couldn't unhappen. "There was a fire," she said. "Your mother is gone." I knew right then it wasn't an accident. They were investigating, she told me. They had found her in the basement. Nothing was left, nothing salvageable anyway. The house was gone. "I'm so sorry," she said. Then she collapsed and began to sob uncontrollably. The sobbing was so intense, I remember feeling more sorry for her than I did for myself.

When I had been living with my grandmother for a few months, she found an old cassette of my mother's voice that had been recorded on my fifth birthday. I played the tape over and over in my room. My mother sounded so happy. "William, half a decade!" she cheered. "William, have a decade!" I cheered back. That was the only thing I said on the tape. "Happy birthday, honey," my mother said. Then she kissed me, which I remembered from that day. I could hear my grandmother in the background. She was nothing like my mother. Instead of flamboyant and vivacious, she was stern and quiet, tolerant, plain spoken. She didn't read much. She preferred the television. Or the radio. She never drank. Maybe she did when she was young. She smoked cigarettes. I forgave her for that, although that's what ultimately did her in.

As life went on, I became more and more interested in art, partly because the only teachers who showed more than a passing interest in me as a person were my art teachers. Other than consorting with them, I mainly kept to myself in my classes. Throughout school, particularly in my teens, I became obsessed with drawing, which left little time for things like, say, desire, let alone the time to go chasing after the actual fulfillment of those desires. Certainly, I was interested in girls. But given my sullen demeanor, there wasn't much hope for me, even if drawing hadn't been my primary distraction. Most of the drawings I did back then were macabre figure studies, some superheroes (including a failed attempt at a graphic novel about sentient garbage trucks), and anatomical studies of birds. I'm not sure where the bird thing came from or what it meant, if anything. It could have just been that I liked drawing feathers. Rendering the barbs in fine detail was a little bit like a musician practicing scales.

My grandmother's house was not far from my original home in West St. Paul. Her house was older, built in the

1910s, and she had inherited it from her mother. It was in a different school district one suburb over, so I didn't have to face all the same kids after the fire. During my senior year in high school, my grandmother died of cancer. She was diagnosed over Christmas break, and within three months she was gone. I had just turned eighteen. The house was sold with the help of some well-meaning guidance counselors, but it wasn't paid for, so most of the money went to the bank. The rest went to tuition at the Minneapolis College of Art and Design.

My decent grades and budding portfolio got me into the competitive school. It was at MCAD that the idea of dating at least became plausible. Drawing was no longer a distraction or a liability. It was an asset, part of the natural order of things. The classes I took provided ample opportunity for me to socialize—more than I could take, really. I wasn't sure why the other students didn't just shut up and paint, but that may never have been their primary reason for being in the studio. For me, painting always came first. Without painting, there was just me, and I wasn't exactly good company. Even my mother seemed to think this during my time there. She visited so rarely I thought maybe I had made a mistake going to art school.

I never once talked about how my mother died with any of my classmates, not even in college. I would, however, happily tell them all the good things about her. And there were plenty of good things, and good days, that my mother and I shared. I remember the Labor Day at the end of our last summer together. We got up that morning and listened to music in the basement first thing. She played her favorites: Joni Mitchell, Sam Cooke, Willie Nelson, Kris Kristofferson. Nothing contemporary, but I was too young to know the difference. The old stereo had vacuum tubes, and I sat there mesmerized by the glow. My mother's admonishment never to touch the tubes made them that much more captivating.

We left the house midmorning to attend the Minnesota State Fair. My mother loved the rides and games in the midway, and that's where we spent most of the day, and most of our money. She won a small teddy bear in a ring toss game, and, because I was already too old for such a bear, she gave it to a toddler girl who was crying her eyes out about something or other. Her parents were young, probably nineteen or twenty at most—practically kids themselves I realized, even then. They laughed in relief when their daughter stopped crying. At the end of the day, I was exhausted, maybe as exhausted as I'd ever been to that point in my life.

I remember the drive home. Just outside the fairgrounds there was a billboard for Diet Dr Pepper. A woman's hand held the bottle, and I remember asking my mother whose hand it was. "A giant," she said. "The biggest woman who ever lived." She burst out laughing. That was the only time I remember her really, truly laughing. She laughed so hard she missed the green light and didn't stop laughing until the car behind us honked. I didn't think it was funny, but I laughed along, at least until the car horn blared. That night, as I was falling asleep, I thought about the crying toddler and the teddy bear. I wondered who the girl would grow up to be, if she would end up happy or end up more like me.

These were the kinds of stories I was willing to share. But the kinds of stories that would have been helpful for me to share were not the kinds of stories I liked to tell. And I had too many questions. Where did my mother's loss of hope come from? Was hope even a factor? Was it something I did or said? Could I have saved her? Beyond all that, there was no way I was ever going to confide in Sara, or anyone else, that I suffered hallucinations, or visitations, or whatever it was I had been experiencing for so many years since my mother's death. I did, of course, relay certain facts. Sara knew I was an orphan. She knew my mother was an artist. She had seen quite a few of my mother's paintings and even seen some photos of her. But that was it. It might have made things better if I had told Sara the whole truth.

CHAPTER 14

IT WAS GNAWING at me that Sara had come over, drunk from her own party, spent the night in my bed, and then, to top it all off, as I lay sleeping, left the key to my apartment on her way out. At least she hadn't left a note. Her notes had always been nasty, brutish, and short ("Shave better." "Drink less, FFS." "Shower please!"), so I could imagine how much one last note might have fucked me up.

A few weeks passed. One afternoon, I happened upon Sara sitting at a table in the TimeWarp as I walked by the front windows. She was playing with the ice in her drink, chatting and laughing with Einstein as if they were off on vacation somewhere. Einstein was sitting with his chin resting on the palm of his hand, giggling along, practically drooling into his beer. I could not believe Sara would come to the TimeWarp under any circumstances, but bringing Einstein with her was a gangster-level insult. I thought about just heading straight up to my apartment, but they did deserve a little visit, I thought, since they had invaded my turf like this. I entered and went up to the bar. I kept one eye on Sara and one eye on the back of Einstein's neck. I ordered three cans of Grain Belt and walked them over to their table.

"Sara, you seem to have forgotten something." I set the beers down on the table but remained standing.

"William, you remember Stan."

"I thought you went by Einstein," I said.

"Only at the store, Bill."

"It's William, not Bill. Mind if I join you?"

"We thought you'd never ask," Einstein said.

I sat down next to Sara.

"Stan was just telling me his ideas about MUSAK," she said.

"The background music company?" I asked.

"But it's not actually a company," Einstein said. "It's more of a secret society, like the Bone and Dagger Club of Yale."

"Skull and Bones," I corrected him.

"Except MUSAK is worse. It started in Virginia around 1890 and originally called itself the Revolutionary Sawmill. They were into subliminal manipulation, and later sub-aural and sub-sensual manipulation decades before it was studied in the academy."

"The academy?" I was glad I couldn't see Sara's face as I was listening to this drivel.

"Some say it was an ancient Roman way of controlling the mind," he continued. "Weaving small strands of copper into wool, for example."

"What does that have to do with music?" I asked.

"They put it in front of the speakers, filling the room with static current."

"Static current," I said, "is an oxymoron." I gulped my beer.

"The negative ions confuse people. They become passive, jingoistic, and xenophobic."

"Is there a waiter in here today?" I asked. "We could order shots."

"Actually, we're gonna take off," Sara said. "Stan has an appointment."

"What about all this Grain Belt?" I asked.

"I'm sure you can polish them off for us," Sara said.

"Good to see you, Bill," Einstein said.

"My name is not Bill."

"See you later, then."

Sara followed him out the door. I told myself I had wanted to be alone in the first place. That I was glad to see them go. I remembered what Dr. Karlsen had said about "Einstein" meaning "one glass" in German. Poor little Albert One Glass, I thought. I pulled a pen from my pocket and scribbled out a poem on a cocktail napkin:

> Poor little Albert One Glass,
> Who failed his sixth-grade math class,
> Turned out to be quite right,
> About the speed of light,
> When squared and multiplied by mass.

It read like the lyrics of one of Einstein's idiotic songs. I crumpled up the napkin and dropped it on the floor. Later, after finishing all the beer, I carried myself as best I could up the stairs to my apartment, hoping the inebriation would inspire another painting. As I walked in the door, I found a jar of titanium pigment had fallen from the shelf and spilled all over the floorboards. Using a large, dry paintbrush, I swept the harmless pigment back into the plastic jar, screwed on the lid, and replaced it on the shelf.

I studied the cardboard Eddie for a minute. Had he witnessed what happened? It was hard to tell. He appeared to know something I didn't. But what? On the easel there was, to my surprise, a finished painting. It was a scene from my childhood, the year we got a white-flocked Christmas tree.

My mother's final Christmas. I had pictures of that tree in a storage box somewhere. I dragged my finger across the still-wet surface. My mother had just been there.

I sat down on the floor and cried. It had been over a year since my last cry. I crossed my legs and leaned forward, covered my head with my hands, and pressed my body into a tight crouch. Soon I felt a hand on my shoulder. I jumped to my feet. There was no one, nothing there at all. I locked the door, lay down on my bed, and begged the Grain Belt to get the better of me and let me sleep.

CHAPTER 15

SIX WEEKS LATER, on the day of the closing reception, it rained on and off for most of the afternoon. From my apartment window, I watched bar patrons scurry from the bus stop into the TimeWarp, trying as hard as they could not to get drenched. I felt assured by their willingness to run toward a bar, even if their impetus was somewhat different than my own.

I made my way down the hallway to the bathroom, no longer shared. No one had yet come to take Pigeonhole's things, and he hadn't been gone long enough to get an eviction notice. All was quiet. In the bathroom, I was met with the sight of brown sewer water backing up into the tub and rising fast. I immediately went upstairs to tell Vernon. He had more clout with the building manager than anyone else.

Vernon's door was propped open, so I leaned in and said, "Vernon, my bathtub is overflowing."

Vernon was sitting on couch his looking at his iPad. "Pigeonhole has returned, I presume?"

"No, thank God. Just some kind of backup."

Vernon picked up his phone and called Enrique, the caretaker, and told him about the bathtub. Enrique said he'd be right over.

"You know, William, I once met Carl Sagan at the University of Tucson. He was discussing the probability of extraterrestrial life in our galaxy. Did I ever tell you about that?"

"Yes."

"No, I didn't."

"I gotta go."

"Well then, maybe another time." Vernon turned his attention to his iPad, and I headed downstairs.

After about twenty minutes, Enrique arrived. By this time, the bathtub was nearly overflowing. He took one look at the rising water and decided he'd better call a real plumber. "Nasty," he said as he held his nose and pulled out his cellphone. When the plumber arrived, he fixed the drain in five minutes with a metal snake.

I decided to stop in at the TimeWarp before walking downtown to the reception. I found Enrique already at the bar. I ordered a whiskey, neat, and Enrique ordered a beer. We faced straight ahead and drank in silence. The TimeWarp was dark, cramped, old, smelly, crusty, and often crowded. There weren't enough bars of its type remaining in Minneapolis, and there were fewer and fewer every year. As soon as one became too popular, a developer would come in and buy the building, at which point that particular bar's days were numbered. The TimeWarp might have met such a fate if the neighborhood had been slightly more appealing to developers. Lucky for me, it wasn't. I tipped my whiskey back and left a dollar bill under the glass. Enrique nodded, and I headed out.

I looked up and down the street, conspicuously, wondering if today would be the day I'd finally see my mother again. I walked down Washington Avenue, past Bobby and Steve's Auto World, past its elevated carousel with a 1957 Chevy spinning in the window, the smell of overcooked hot dogs and gasoline drifting through the neighborhood. I could imagine my mother behind the wheel of that spinning Chevy, but there was no sight of her. Nor was she in the taxi driving past me. She wasn't in the window of the wholesale florist, though I could imagine her there as well, picking petals off the snapdragons and orchids, tucking them into her hair, maybe eating them, or putting them in her pocket for later.

Above me was a billboard, an advertisement for pillows. How long it had been since I had purchased a new pillow? In fact, I couldn't remember purchasing a pillow to begin with. Where did pillows come from? The sky? A piece of garbage tumbled across the street in a light wind. I envied it. It was going with the flow. Hurting no one. Not being stubborn or wishing for too much. Eventually, someone would pick it up. That person would feel better about themself for having done so. The garbage would have helped someone feel better while itself being noticed and taken care of. Even garbage had something on me. I kept walking.

The blocks went by with no sign of my mother. For a late Friday afternoon, both pedestrian and car traffic were lighter than usual. Monday was Memorial Day, and many people had already left town. I turned north on Portland Avenue toward the Mississippi River, finally admitting to myself that I was actively searching for my mother. When I was young, I learned that I would have to carry my own weight, and that I should not, in so many words, go looking for mommy. Of course, I knew there would never be a father, no male authority, no one to pick up the slack when she let go of her parental responsibilities, which was often. I didn't learn all this on my own. She simply told me: "Be self-sufficient. Be agile. Be vigilant." Strange advice for a child. When she died, I realized this advice was not universal. Just the opposite. It was tailor-made for me, specific to what she knew my needs would be, whether then or years later.

I continued down Portland toward the river. A small commercial van parked in a desolate lot advertised Free Needle Exchange. Used Needles for Sterile, No Questions Asked. I wondered if they knew Pigeonhole, though I didn't stop to ask. As I passed by, I wished for a van offering the kind of exchange I needed—trading out the thoughts in my head for something clean and new. Free Thought Exchange. Used Thoughts for Sterile, No Questions Asked.

I strolled out onto the Stone Arch Bridge. It was clear where some of the people had gone. The late afternoon sun fell across the faces and bodies of these tired but seemingly satisfied professional people. There were a few idiots on in-line skates, some wearing headphones, and one person was painting a horrid version of the lock and dam in watercolor. There was a man sitting on a 5-gallon bucket, busking with a harmonica. He had collected quite a bit of cash in a small suitcase.

There might have been two hundred people or more out on the bridge enjoying the weather. The mood was one of leaving the workplace behind and letting the moment, not to mention the Mississippi River, carry everything away. Spring had arrived in full force, and it was time to celebrate. I hadn't come for that exact reason, but I realized I had little choice but to participate. I, too, had reason to celebrate, or at least I hoped I did. Though I hadn't heard it directly from Caroline, Vernon let me know that my show had been successful.

I stood staring at the city skyline as if staring at a broken vase. Or was I the broken one? Did it even matter? There was nothing to be done. No amount of therapy, no amount of alcohol, no amount of sobriety, no scientific understanding, no course of study, religion, or belief could have helped. There was only my mother and me, and neither of us had an adequate answer to what was happening. People milled around us unaffected.

"I'm so tired." I had not intended to say this out loud. My utterance caught the attention of a woman farther on, across the bike path from me. She looked away, pulling out her phone, possibly to distract herself or to show me that someone she knew might be arriving any minute.

I turned back to see my mother. Immediately, she turned away, starting toward downtown. I watched her walk off, smoldering, trailing ash, occasionally glancing back at me as if beckoning me to follow. I decided the other direction was better. I made my way toward Sara's apartment. I hadn't intended to go there, not consciously, but I found myself in front of her building with no desire to be anywhere else.

This could go a few different ways, I thought. Sara could be looking out the window, and that would be a problem. But it would have to be dark out and I would have to be drunk for it to really be a problem. Still, I was just standing there looking at her building, right at her window. The blinds were closed. I was okay for the moment. But Sara could also be coming home, possibly looking at me right now from another vantage point. Regardless, in any scenario the question remained: What was I doing there?

I approached the building's front door. All the labels on the buzzers had fallen off. I wasn't positive which one was hers. I thought this might prevent me from actually ringing one of them, something I was dreading to do, but knew I eventually would. It was getting closer to sunset, and the warmth of evening light gave me an idea. I could add a slight red tint to the varnish I had been using on my paintings. It might make my work a little less stark, a bit friendlier. A painting could be your friend if the light was right, I thought. I looked over the buzzers again. I wanted to talk to the buzzers, ask which one of them was hers, and have one of them answer, "Well, it's me, silly, third from the left. Do you want me to ring myself?"

I ran my fingers along the buttons, hoping muscle memory would lead me to the right one. It didn't. I would have to press a button or leave. I closed my eyes and pressed one. I waited a full minute. No one answered.

Chapter 16

I ARRIVED AT the gallery an hour late. Being late for my own show was preferable to involving myself in forced conversations about my artwork with people I didn't know, especially people who were never going to buy anything and were mainly in the way of the people who might. I had a quick spiel prepared that I modified as needed to suit practically any question about my work: "I've stopped making academic art-school art. I'm still experimenting, of course, but I'm not interested in exercises in theory anymore." All of which meant nothing—less than nothing, really, if it's possible to speak words that somehow remove meaning. If I had said that the root word of painting was "pain," that would have been closer to the truth, at least for me. And I kept it to myself that my paint moved across the canvas on its own, that my brushes fell off the table over and over, that my compositions were reworked for the better as I slept. I kept it to myself that there were masterstrokes in my paintings that I hadn't made, couldn't have made, didn't know how to make.

Walking through the crowd to the adjunct gallery, with its tall windows, its patinated floorboards, its ornate fleur-de-lis-patterned iron grate in the center of the floor, I could see that the space was indeed perfect for my paintings, as perfect as any room could be, lending them a degree of credibility they might not otherwise have had. Most of the paintings were desolate suburban landscapes with a solitary house in the middle ground, all in various states of combustion. I painted them in dark hues and bold, crisp lines. I covered them all in semigloss varnish, which gave them a fishing-lure kind of luster. Perfect for the Land of 10,000 Lakes.

Back in the main gallery, Vernon stood next to the hors d'oeuvres pouring himself a glass of sparkling wine. He drank it quickly, and just as quickly poured himself another. Crowded rooms bothered him and ruined his appetite, so he drank his way through his receptions. But, because Vernon was funny when drunk, he was popular with the gallery-goers in town. He was always invited to receptions, and he attended most of them. Bumping elbows for a few hours was an unavoidable occupational hazard, apparently, for both of us. At least he made the most of it.

Forging a path through the crush of people waiting to banter with Vernon would have been too difficult, so instead I looked around for anyone else I knew. Just then someone tapped me on the shoulder. It was Caroline.

"You're late."

"Because I was having a panic attack. I promise I'll stay until at least ten o'clock."

"Here, drink this." She handed me a glass of wine. "I've got some news for you."

"About sales?"

"Yes, that." Caroline then spotted an important collector, someone even I recognized, and without another word she took off in her direction.

A moment later Sara walked in from the street with Einstein right behind her. I panicked and darted into the storage room, closing the door behind me. The storage room had a window facing the alley, a window just large enough for me to crawl through. I finished the glass of wine first, then opened the window and squirmed out. I walked around to the front of the gallery and remained outside for several minutes watching Sara and Einstein through the windows.

Vernon spotted me and came outside.

"Congratulations, William."

"For?"

"Caroline didn't tell you? Every one of your paintings sold."

Every one of my mother's paintings, I wanted to correct him. "I was looking for red dots, but I didn't see any."

"Caroline doesn't use those. She likes the element of mystery. At any rate, if she pays you in a timely manner—a big if, by the way—you should have enough money to pay your rent for a year. Not bad!"

I had never bothered to add up what a sellout might amount to, but I realized Vernon was right. I wasn't sure Caroline would pay me on time—she was notorious for being on the slow side to pay her artists—but at least I had something to look forward to.

Sara saw me through the window. I tried to move behind Vernon to avoid her, but she immediately headed outside with Einstein in tow. There was nowhere to hide. Sensing danger, Vernon slipped away and went back inside.

"Bill!" Einstein shouted. "Long time, no see. Love your paintings. The red skies. The flames. Really awesome." Einstein couldn't handle awkward conversations, but he was a far better liar than I had imagined. Either that, or he was actually impressed.

"Congratulations, William," Sara said. "You got an incredible amount of work done in a really short time." Instead of raising her glass of wine in my honor, she handed it to me. I gladly accepted it.

"I'm a little surprised to see you two here," I said.

"Wouldn't want to miss it," Einstein said. This was a worse lie. "By the way, there's another reception up the street at Instant Space tonight. Guess who we saw?"

I turned to Sara, expecting her to answer.

"No, seriously, guess," Einstein demanded. "You'll never guess."

"Um, Richard Hell?"

"Close. Your old neighbor. Pigeontoe or whatever."

I scratched my head. "So he's out of the hospital? But why would he be at an art show?"

"He was in a wheelchair," Sara said, "playing an acoustic guitar. He even sang a little."

"Surprisingly decent voice," Einstein added.

"He looked good, too," Sara continued. "He was wearing a big, blue crucifix around his neck. And he mentioned you in one of his songs."

I had never heard Pigeonhole sing. I was worried this was all a nightmare. I smelled the wine in my glass. It smelled real enough, so I drank it down.

"The lyrics were something like, 'He forced me to hit rock bottom, by tossing false idols like napalm.'" Sara grinned, a beautiful sight, something I hadn't seen her do in months.

Talk about rock bottom. I wasn't going to stand around and gab with Einstein and Sara. I had to get away from them, process this information about Pigeonhole somewhere alone. There was no need for me to stay and schmooze. All the paintings were sold.

"Thanks for coming," I said. "Good to see you both." I, too, was lying. "I need to run and talk to Caroline for a minute."

I moved away, down the sidewalk, to the edge of the large gallery windows, pretending to look for Caroline. It was starting to sink in. This sellout was big deal. It meant more shows and more collectors asking about my work between shows. The ideal situation. I owed my mother big time. I turned down the alley and headed home, carrying the wine glass with me all the way.

Back at my apartment, I summoned enough energy to begin the painting of my mother I had planned to start weeks earlier. I had built and stretched a door-sized canvas with this portrait in mind. It was too tall to put on the easel, so I propped it up against the wall between the windows. I had made a few preliminary sketches, but decided not to consult them. I wanted to begin from the beginning. I opened my box of paints and, against my better judgment, began by painting my mother's face in the center of the canvas. Next I sketched a vintage yellow dress, bare legs and feet, knees caked with dirt from the garden, one hand in a fist, the other clutching a bouquet of dried flowers. It was raining. My mother stood in her own shadow gripping the water collecting in her palms, as if the water itself was flowing so furiously that if she released her grip, she would flash away in a flood right then and there.

I painted her standing on a tree stump at the edge of a ravine, burned trees and a barbed-wire fence in the background, singed grass, mud and ash below, a maroon sky and dull moon poking through the rain clouds above. A car in the mid-distance, an old silver Toyota Camry, was the car that had burned in our garage the day she set our house on fire. In the back window of the car, a child could be seen—a small child looking right at her with a broken smile. When I got to this point, I realized it was five o'clock in the morning.

CHAPTER 17

WILLIAM—WHEN HE was very young, maybe just four or five—would sleep for twelve or more hours a night. After putting him to bed at six-thirty, he might still be sound asleep at seven the next morning. I had to wake him for pre-school, and I would always wait until the last minute. When I caressed his cheek and spoke softly into his ear, he would look up at me and say something like, "But, Mom, I just fell asleep." I could only laugh. "It's morning already," I would say. But he wouldn't believe me. "Same as yesterday, same as tomorrow. Time to get up."

He may not remember, but during those long hours of deep sleep, I would sit in his room and read to him for hours on end. Sylvia Plath, Virginia Woolf, Louise Erdrich, Toni Morrison, Emily Dickinson, Doris Lessing, Joyce Carol Oates, Maya Angelou, Joan Didion, Flannery O'Connor, Anaïs Nin, Gertrude Stein, Shirley Jackson. I did not allow men into the house if I could avoid it, and that included their words. Men—through their words and thoughts and actions—would find their way to William eventually. Why rush such things? And, besides, the words of these and other women were, like the women themselves, so full of force and wit and depth, I couldn't bear to spend my precious time in the company of anyone else.

By the time he was seven, those long nights were coming to an end. He'd stir when I read aloud and wouldn't fall into a deep sleep until I stopped. It was difficult giving up the ritual. I had been reading to him for years. The words had found their way into his psyche. Exactly when those words and ideas might come back out again in another form was different matter. For the time being, at least, rest was the most important thing for him. In fact, rest might be the most important thing there is. Rest—something I was never any good at. I believe I passed this trait onto my son. He's so preoccupied with his day-to-day life, his interests, his conflicts, his relationships. I was never much interested in all that. And then there's Sara. Does William really love her? So it seems. Otherwise, why go to all that trouble? But he does seem obsessed. She, however, does not have this problem. She knows how to move on, or at least how to keep moving forward.

On the other hand, William is unique. If there was someone worthy of being obsessed over, it would be William. There's so much more to him than I could have ever dreamed of. His eye for color is a gift, something that can be uncovered and nurtured, but, like perfect pitch in music, can't be taught. His color choices in his best paintings tell a story of their own, an emotional, visceral story within a pictorial one. That was something I could only dream of achieving when I was alive. Beyond that, he has a knack for the materiality of paint. He isn't afraid of it. He doesn't try to impose his will on it. He lets the paint be paint the way a poet lets words be words on the page. But not a jumble of words, not words for the sake of words. How he does this with paint while not drawing attention to it I may never understand.

I wish I could hear his voice. But I haven't heard a voice since the day I died. And I can barely speak myself. One voice I never heard, even when I was alive, was the voice of my own father. He died before I was born, supposedly of a heart attack, at age thirty. My mother never talked about him, never remarried, never even considered it. I grew up, in a way, just as William did, with no men in the house, no siblings, just a mother. But my mother somehow survived it, unlike me. That wasn't so surprising, really. Most people can do that. The surprising part, to me, was that for her it somehow wasn't a struggle. That fact allowed me to put enough faith in her to take care of William when I no longer could.

She did not raise a weak child in me. My struggle wasn't one of weakness. Yet I wasn't strong enough to spend any significant time with her after the fire. I don't know why. Maybe I *was* weak. Or maybe I was saving all my strength for something else. Something even my own mother couldn't have survived.

CHAPTER 18

I SLEPT MOST of the next day. When I awoke, the cardboard Eddie had been knocked over, and significant changes to the painting had been made. The car was gone, but the boy was still there, no longer smiling, and now standing alone near the edge of the ravine. The sky was redder, and the tree stump was replaced by a garden of lilies. My mother's face had changed as well. She looked older, thinner, sadder. She still held dried flowers in one hand, but in the other she held an unlit match. I decided I didn't want any more of her help with this painting, or really any painting. From then on, I kept the painting covered with a sheet when I wasn't working on it. I added metal clamps so there would be no confusion about my desire to finish the painting on my own.

Early evening arrived, and I sat on the edge of my bed staring at my TV. After a minute, I turned it on, along with my ancient VCR. On the night of the service station fire, I had taped the late news coverage. I played the tape often. So often, in fact, that I could see the fire in my mind when I closed my eyes. I put the tape into the machine again and watched news anchor Dale Frank of Channel 8, the man with the gaudy house on Lake of the Isles, coldly report on the incident. "The service station was closed at the time of the explosion. A small fire from an unknown source caused an improperly serviced propane tank to explode, setting the pumps ablaze. One firefighter was treated for smoke inhalation. No other injuries were reported."

I turned off the TV. I felt the urge to slip into my pajamas and go to bed early. Just then I remembered something I had left at Sara's apartment. My old robe, a Pendleton. I wanted it back. I had the urge to go over and demand it back. Obviously this was a terrible idea. And obviously I would try it the very next night.

I spent most of the next day drifting in and out of a light sleep. I wasn't in the mood to work on the painting or to start a new one. The day frittered itself away until, just before dusk, I left for Sara's apartment with a mind to, at the very least, send a message that I was no longer merely another failed artist. I was a somewhat less failed artist with a vintage Pendleton robe, and I wanted it back.

At her building door, the names on the buzzers had been replaced. Hers was, in fact, the third one over. But, of course, I still had my keys. I entered casually, but with conviction, and bounded up the stairs. Once in front of her door, I debated my next move. The only thing to do was knock or leave. A moment later the knob turned and the door swung open.

"I had the weirdest feeling you were out here," Sara said.

"Why?"

"I sensed your lack of conviction. Can I have my keys, please?"

I handed them to her.

"By the way, what are you doing here, unannounced, again?"

"I was just in the neighborhood, so I thought I'd stop by."

Right then, Einstein came from the bedroom to the living room carrying a bong in one hand and a tall stack of vinyl records in the other. Incense burned on the coffee table next to two glasses of wine and a nearly empty bottle. He was wearing the robe.

"Wow, Bill! I thought you were the pizza guy," he squawked.

"My name is not Bill, and I am not the pizza guy."

"Well, did you see the pizza guy? Because man, are we starving! I'm telling you, man, are we starving!"

"Get out of my robe."

"Your robe?" He set the records down on the floor next to scores of others. "Sara said it was hers."

I turned to Sara who was staring at me as if I were a ghost myself.

"William," Sara started, "you really need to go."

I moved past Sara and into the living room.

"My Pendleton," I said. "Give it to me."

"Fine. I'll be right back. Don't touch these," Einstein said, neatening the air above the stack of records with a tai-chi-like gesture. "They're all first-issue."

"Actually, never mind," I said. "You can keep it." I didn't know why I said that. I definitely wanted it back.

"Goddamn it, William." Sara threw her keys at me. "Will you just get out of here?"

"All right," I said. "I'm walking out the door. This is it. This is me walking out the door. As if I were never even here. As if it were your robe all along. Which it isn't."

Sara said nothing. I continued backwards until I was out the door and nearly across the hall. Sara walked up to the door and slammed it shut.

"Wow, you really told her," Clarissa said from down the hall.

"What are you doing here?"

"I moved into the building last week. I'm one floor up. I can hear everything that goes on down here," she said.

"Everything?"

"I'm afraid so. I could tell you some things."

"Please don't," I said.

"You're never going to let this go, are you?" she asked.

"You mean the robe?"

"You know what I mean. You're not here for the robe."

She was right. I wasn't going to let it go.

"I think I better go home," I said.

"Good thinking," Clarissa said, shaking her head, mocking me. "For a change."

CHAPTER 19

NEARLY THREE MONTHS passed, and I did not hear from Sara the entire time, nor did I attempt any communication with her. Pigeonhole's apartment had been cleared out by a group that appeared to be from an evangelical church, judging from the giant cross painted on their van.

Around this time, I began work on a portrait of Sara. I worked from a photo I had taken of her early in our relationship. She was sitting in Mickey's Diner in St. Paul eating a hamburger. No one could eat a hamburger like Sara. Watching her put away a burger was like watching a professional basketball player dunk a ball from the free throw line: first came disbelief, then awe, and finally jealousy. Of course she knew that burgers aren't exactly healthy, but she also knew how good they can be for your soul. A great burger could, in her opinion, prevent a psychotic break, avert a midlife crisis, or keep the peace in a relationship. If only the occasional cheeseburger could have kept the peace in ours.

I remember what she said after finishing that particular burger that night. It was well after midnight, and we were the only two people in the 24-hour diner. She took a sip of her Diet Coke, clapped her hands together, burped audibly, and said, "I could never be a vegetarian."

"No one's a vegetarian," I said. "They're all faking."

"Let's hope so."

She signaled the waitress, and for a split second, I thought she was going to order another burger. But she just wanted the check because she didn't want to miss the last train back to Minneapolis. That was when I pulled out my camera, a little Ricoh point-and-shoot I liked to carry around. The expression of righteousness on her face was captured perfectly in the photograph, but capturing it on canvas seriously tested the limits of my ability as a painter. I spent a great deal of time trying to get the tilt of her eyebrows just right, the line of her lips to look remotely true to life.

After working for a few nights in a row on the portrait, I set it aside. It was making my mind feel swollen and blunted, as if I might forget who she was, forget why I was painting her in the first place. At that point, I wanted my mother to finish the painting for me, but I had the strangest feeling this was one she'd never touch.

Eventually, Caroline sent me $4,000, with a promise to pay the remaining amount within a few weeks. In the meantime, I had been painting steadily, and Caroline was taking work and selling the pieces one by one. I checked the mail obsessively, sometimes multiple times a day, for anything from Caroline.

One afternoon, on my third mailbox run of the day, I found an envelope with my name and address handwritten in India ink. I tore it open, assuming it was another check. I nearly gagged when I saw that it was an invitation to the wedding of Pigeonhole and Tanya, taking place in just two weeks. To my further mortification, there was to be a special performance by Pigeonhole at the reception. I wondered who had sent me the invitation. Could it have been Pigeonhole himself? Was this an olive branch? Or maybe Tanya had mailed it. The handwriting on the envelope gave little away, but I couldn't imagine either one of them printing so neatly.

On the back of the invitation was a QR code. I scanned it. It led to a YouTube channel called, simply, Pigeonhole. Amazingly, he had more than 100,000 followers. What on earth? I watched a few of his videos. Most began with a prayer led by Pigeonhole dubbed over intense shredding. He would then go into a tutorial regarding the finer details of that particular shred. The comments adorned him with praise from all over the world—London, Hong Kong, Kolkata, Melbourne, Buenos Aires, and, of course, Minneapolis. It appeared he was becoming an internet sensation, at least within a particular subculture of guitar shredding fandom that I hadn't realized existed.

I closed the app and let the all-too-familiar sounds of Pigeonhole's playing recede from my mind. The smile on the cardboard Eddie now seemed weirdly sinister. I put him back in the closet. The invitation had no other information and, strangely, no way to RSVP. But it didn't matter. There was no question I would attend, and somehow there was no question in my mind that Sara and Einstein would be there, too.

Chapter 20

IN THE TERRITORIAL sense, I always considered the Time-Warp my bar—which seemed fair, since I lived above it—but Sara and I had never discussed it as such. And, because I had run into Sara and Einstein once there already, I was forced to scan the bar for them every single time I entered, and repeatedly while drinking. I dreaded the thought of them showing up and testing my wits at the end of a long night. But I actually hoped I'd see them there again, just to get it over with.

About a week before the wedding, instead of Sara, it was Clarissa who showed up at the TimeWarp. She was standing at the door alone. She gave me a quick wave and turned back to wait for someone at the door. Through the windows I saw Dr. Karlsen in his BMW. He was an expert parallel parker, which did not surprise me in the least.

Dr. Karlsen was wearing a perfectly tailored three-piece suit in dark gray, a red polka-dot tie, and a matching handkerchief in his breast pocket. Dressed this way, he seemed to be from another time—possibly the future, but more likely the past—a time that could teach us all a valuable lesson if only we would pay closer attention to the way we dress. Clarissa was wearing what appeared to be a jogging outfit, bright yellow, with white sneakers and a black bandanna on her head. She must have been coming from the gym. The contrast with Dr. Karlsen's suit made him seem all the more elegant.

"How did you find me?" I asked Clarissa.

"You checked in on Facebook."

"I'm not even on Facebook." I was on my fourth drink and was a bit worried that I might come across as either ridiculous or sad. "Am I?"

"We took a shot in the dark," Dr. Karlsen said.

"Please, sit down," I said, gesturing to the two open barstools next to me.

"I was thinking," Dr. Karlsen said as he took a seat, "that maybe you could join Clarissa and me for dinner sometime."

"Where, here?" I asked, surprised.

"No, no. At my house," he said. "I've—" he paused, looking at Clarissa, "we've missed you."

"Just the two of you?" I asked. "No Sara?"

"No Sara," Dr. Karlsen assured me. "I'd like to show you some of the artwork I've been collecting lately. And you definitely need to see the Clarks station. It's been completely rebuilt. You'd never know about the fire by looking at it."

"It's *Clark*, not Clarks. And it's not a Clark anymore. It's a BP," Clarissa said.

"It was Clarks for twenty years!"

I didn't want to lose focus, but I couldn't help but think about the videotape of the fire. I had watched that gas station burn so many times I couldn't imagine seeing the station intact again. What would my mother think?

Just then, I glanced over to see my mother outside, leaning against the window, her hands cupped around her eyes, her face pressed to the glass. She had impeccable timing.

"Brass tacks, William," Clarissa said, leaning in. "We found out that Pigeonhole invited you to his wedding. He also invited Sara and Stan. We're thinking maybe you should skip it."

"But I already RSVP'd."

"That's a lie," Clarissa said.

My mother was still at the window but had turned around to face the street. I could see her twiddling her thumbs behind her back. She was excited about the wedding, I could tell.

Dr. Karlsen turned to look. Of course, there was nothing for him to see. He stood, preparing to leave. "I'm afraid we need to run. But think about our proposal. Both proposals, in fact." Considering the wedding, I found his use of the word "proposal" to be delightful, and I'm sure he did, too.

I stood up and offered my hand. He shook it.

"I'll text you some dates," Clarissa said. "What's your number?"

I gave it to her. "My calendar is wide open," I said.

With that, they turned and left. At the door, Clarissa stopped in her tracks and spun back around. She marched up to me and leaned in again, a bit too close this time.

"What have you been looking at?" She pointed to the window. "Over there."

I was unsure whether or not to acknowledge her question.

"Just keeping an eye out. Old habit."

"Old habit?" She took a step back. "I've heard those die hard." She turned around and joined her father again.

I wasn't sure how to feel about this meeting, the way they had sought me out to uninvite me to Pigeonhole's wedding. But I did feel honored that Dr. Karlsen would go to all this trouble to deliver his message in person, while also inviting me to dinner at his house again on top of it. And while I was pretty certain I would take him up on the dinner invitation, I was absolutely certain I would attend Pigeonhole's wedding.

CHAPTER 21

BY THE TIME the wedding day arrived, I had dragged myself through several thrift stores looking for a passable outfit. I ultimately settled on a late-'70s lime green three-piece suit, an off-white broadcloth shirt, and a red polka-dot tie just like Dr. Karlsen's. I got the suit dry-cleaned in hopes of removing a reddish-brown stain on the lapel, but the stain—possibly ketchup—was merely faded by the cleaning. I covered it with an old Mondale/Ferraro button of similar vintage.

When I arrived at the church, I entered and scanned the pews. Clarissa got my attention with a quick wave. I walked over and sat beside her. Clarissa was wearing a tiered, navy blue satin dress with a high neckline, ankle length, with short ruffled sleeves. Something Sara would never be seen in—she would call it something like "old-lady boring"—but it was just the right mix of festive and formal.

"Bride or groom?" I asked.

"Neither," she said. "I'm only here for the spectacle of it all."

"Where are Sara and Einstein?"

"Not here yet, I guess. I came alone."

I scanned the program. There would be two songs (neither by Pigeonhole), then a poem read by Pigeonhole's uncle Gary, then the vows, and later a reception at the Sanitation Worker's Legion Hall.

"This is going to be horrible," I said.

"That's because what you think of as horrible, other people find wonderful."

The music started. The pews were just about full as the bridesmaids and groomsmen entered the church and moved down the aisle to the altar. Then came the groom himself. Pigeonhole entered the nave in his wheelchair, wearing a crushed velvet blue tuxedo. The bell-bottom pants, too long by several inches, mostly hid his bare feet. He was being pushed by a similarly dressed man who joined the other groomsmen at the altar.

Most of the congregation stood as Tanya entered. She wore a flowing pale yellow gown in the subtlest of floral prints. Her eyes were weepy and hopeful. A few people began to sob. She strode down the aisle alone and took Pigeonhole's hand when she reached the altar. Before I sat down, I caught a glimpse of my mother standing at the back of the nave.

The minister swept into the sanctuary from a side door. She held a manila folder in one hand, her eyeglasses in the other. She thanked everyone for coming, and we all nodded back at her. She told us that this was a very special day and that two lives were becoming one. From the wobbly lectern, Pigeonhole's uncle Gary read a poem by Rainer Maria Rilke. The vows were next. Pigeonhole's voice trembled as he spoke of loving Tanya for all eternity. Finally, the minister pronounced them married, and they kissed. Tanya sat in Pigeonhole's lap, and everyone laughed, everyone but me. A recorded cello accompanied the couple as they made their way out of the church.

"Fast ceremony," I said to Clarissa. "I've brushed my teeth for longer. Did Sara miss it?"

She scanned the church. "I guess so. Maybe they'll be at the reception. By the way," she continued, "Stan is moving to northern Wisconsin next month. He's closing his store and will supposedly be working at a resort up in the woods, emceeing events. It's bizarre, but I guess he's tired of running a business. Sara's thinking about moving up there, too."

I practically fell over. "That's fucking ridiculous. Sara would never move to a resort in the woods." My head was spinning.

"She already gave notice at her job."

"She was going to do that anyway," I said.

"I think it sounds nice up there. They make their own electricity and grow organic food. They even have sheep for wool and cheese and stuff. It's almost like a commune, but for profit."

"I'm not sure what I really saw in Sara in the first place."

"Even though you are clearly still in love with her."

"Am not."

"Do you admit, William," Clarissa fixed her gaze on me, "that you rarely leave your apartment and that a cardboard cutout is your main conversation partner?"

"That has nothing to do with Sara. And is none of your business. And isn't true. And how do you know about that?"

She took her eyes off me and sent them rolling toward the church's painted ceiling. My mother was in the rafters, but of course only I could see her. She had wedged herself between two of the wooden beams that appeared to my untrained eye to be more decorative than structural, and I worried she'd come crashing down on top of us. But then again, maybe she didn't weigh anything. I took a deep breath of the damp church air and felt my lungs going into spasm. I gasped as if I were drowning. My mother, looking down at me intently, appeared to be crying, wiping her eyes. I wanted to ask her if she always cried at weddings.

"Are you okay?" Clarissa asked.

I definitely wasn't. "This should be a happy moment," I said. "For them, I mean. But of course, for me, it isn't."

"When was the last time you were happy?"

"Thursday?"

"Bullshit." Clarissa tugged at my lapel. "Mondale?"

"It came with the suit," I lied.

"1980 was the real stolen election," she said.

"How so?"

"Reagan stole our future. Anyway, do you need a ride to the reception?"

"No," I said. "I drove."

"Me too," she said. "I guess I'll see you there."

Dozens of sewer workers and scores of relatives had filled the Sanitation Workers' Legion Hall by the time I arrived. Food was being served on a gigantic round buffet. I waited my turn in line for the blackened Cajun seitan and artichoke heart kabobs. A hired wedding band was tuning up on stage. The program said the band would be playing two sets with a musical interlude by Pigeonhole. I went over to the bar to order a drink. Clarissa found me there. We each got a Mai Tai.

"Vic Bergeron invented the Mai Tai for Trader Vic's, his restaurant in Oakland," Clarissa said. "'Mai Tai' means 'out of this world' in Tahitian."

"How do you know all that?"

"I know all about drinks."

Yet another contrast to Sara, who knew nothing about alcohol, other than that she liked it. The band began to play.

"Want to dance?" Clarissa asked me.

I was taken aback by the offer, but I could hardly have said no under the circumstances. We finished our drinks and stepped out onto the dance floor. It was loud and dark. I didn't see Sara or Einstein anywhere. The band, which claimed to change its name for every gig and that night was going by California Emission, started with "Take Me Home, Country Roads." Clarissa was all smiles, twirling, enjoying herself as if her entire life was just this one moment. The next song was "Hey Jude." Clarissa decided this song called for a series of slow, almost sultry dance moves. Her eyes were closed, but she moved around me as if she knew every move I would make before I did. The song went on so long I could hardly stand it, so I suggested to Clarissa that we head back to the bar.

"I'll take another Mai Tai," I told the bartender. The bartender, who appeared to be heavily intoxicated, scratched her head, then began to work on the drink. The song ended, and Pigeonhole's uncle got up on stage. The bartender handed me the strongest drink I could have hoped for.

"Ladies and gentlemen," Pigeonhole's uncle said into the microphone, "thank you so much for coming tonight. I'm a very proud uncle. Harry is like a son to me. When I heard about the accident, I was crushed. But since that day, Harry has found a new path. We're all eternally grateful. In that light, we now have a very special treat for you. A guitar hero in the making ... everyone's favorite axe-wielding metalhead ... please give it up for ... Pigeonhole!"

There was an explosion of cheers and applause. The lights went dim, and an impressive amount of dry ice fog filled the stage. Then I heard it—that old familiar hum. A few seconds later Pigeonhole emerged, churning out a cascade of notes as Tanya rolled him and his amp to center stage.

Pigeonhole mesmerized the crowd with his soloing as I hung my head and prepared to weep. I had not heard his guitar playing live since the night of the fall. It wasn't something I was emotionally prepared to reexperience. After a few cringe-filled minutes, I could take no more and headed outside. Clarissa followed.

"Too much for you?" The look on her face was one of actual concern, so much so that I became concerned for myself.

"Everything is too much for me," I said.

"Or not enough," she added correctly. "You don't really have to tell me if you don't want to, but I'd like to know something."

For some reason I took this to mean she already knew something but just wanted to confirm her belief. "What do you want to know?"

"I want to know what's always bothering you. It's like, you're always staring off into space or looking for something. You're not the typical tortured artist. You actually seem like you're being tortured in real time."

I said nothing. This was not supposed to be happening. What I wanted was for Clarissa to explain to me exactly what I had to do to get Sara back and exactly how Einstein was going to be humiliated and then eliminated from the picture.

After several seconds of me staring at her, she said, "I've enjoyed getting to know you, by the way. I think you're a fantastic artist. I think Sara made a mistake. I just wanted you to know."

Again, I said nothing. She paused a moment, then turned to walk back inside. I didn't stop her. I stared up at the cold night sky. In a few minutes, California Emission retook the stage. I finished my drink but stayed outside. Soon,

Pigeonhole came rolling out the door with Tanya following. He had his guitar in his lap. His amplifier was rolling on casters behind him, attached to his chair with a steel chain.

"Dudeman! I'm glad to see you. I wanted to apologize."

"Apologize?" I was shocked. "For what?"

"For all the noise, and for not cleaning the bathroom, and for the—"

I cut him off. "I'm sorry, too."

"You mean for throwing my cardboard Eddie down the stairs?"

"Yeah, that. And ..."

"And causing me to almost kill myself?"

"Yeah, that, too. Especially that. I'm sorry about all of it."

"Dudeman, if anything, you helped bring about the spiritual overhaul I had so desperately postponed. That ambulance ride was like Christmas Past, Christmas Present, and Chris Kringle all in one trip. I saw myself in the rearview mirror of life, and I wasn't any closer than I appeared. I needed help, and God answered the call." He mimed making a phone call.

Tanya added, "In other words, if it weren't for your cruel insensitivity and intolerance of human frailty, we might both be dead."

"The Lord works in mysterious ways, Dudeman. I've got much physical therapy ahead of me and several surgeries. But there is hope." He made the sign of the cross. They both laughed. "But seriously, dude," Pigeonhole said. "If you're ever in need of anything by way of the Holy Spirit, don't hesitate to reach out. I'm on TikTok now."

"He already has 80,000 followers," Tanya interjected. "Anyway, we have to get going. We have a paying gig in Des Moines tomorrow, and it's going to be a long drive. The honeymoon is over."

I was impressed by their dedication. Pigeonhole offered his hand, and I shook it. "God bless you, artist dude!" With that, he rolled off with Tanya. The party inside continued as if the guests of honor had never left the building.

I was lost, woozy, in a place beyond words. I could hear California Emission kicking off their second set with "Ring of Fire." My drink and the cool evening air had left my lips numb. My teeth began to chatter. I stepped over to the bushes and threw up. Then I staggered back inside to look for Sara.

In the men's room, I rinsed my mouth and tried to straighten myself out. It was a struggle to look in the mirror. My eyes were bloodshot and my lips chapped, but I attempted to make myself presentable. A minute or so later, I returned to the dance floor. Sara and Einstein were cheek to cheek, slow-dancing to "Lady in Red." I shuffled up to them and tapped Einstein on the shoulder.

"Can I cut in?" I slurred.

They stopped. Stan gave me an intimidating grimace. He then pulled my tie and said, "I don't think we can be friends anymore. Got it?"

I slapped him lightly on the cheek, mainly to get him to let go of my tie. This drew the attention of a few of the sanitation workers, who came over, I assumed, to quell the situation.

"All right, a fight!" one of them said.

"My money's on the bald guy," another said.

"It's more of a receding hairline," I said back.

"I'd say you're just plain bald, Bill," Stan said.

I took aim at Einstein with my fist. But it was too late. I was, in fact, going bald. The room started to spin. I lost my balance and tipped over backwards. I hit the floor, and all the sanitation workers moaned. The band stopped playing. Einstein stood over me, his mop of hair looking like a corona lit from behind by the stage lights. He pulled his foot back. I prepared to be struck in the leg or ribs. But before Einstein was able to deliver a blow, Sara stepped in front of him. She led him off the dance floor, and I struggled to my feet. Clarissa waved me over to the bar. The adrenaline helped me keep my balance as I crossed the dance floor. The band began again with "It's Still Rock and Roll to Me."

"That could have been worse," Clarissa said.

"How so?"

"Well, it could always be worse," she said.

"I need to get out of here."

"I can take you home. You're in no condition to get yourself there."

"Thanks," I said. "You were right. I should have skipped the wedding. Actually, I should have known better myself."

"Nah, it's better this way."

"Why?"

"Because this way I can be right forever."

Part Two

CHAPTER 22

EARLY ON A Friday evening, two months after the wedding, I sent Clarissa a text asking to meet me at the TimeWarp. I needed information—information I was certain Clarissa had, information I believed she wanted to share, given the opportunity. She, always quick to text back, responded nearly instantly saying she could meet in an hour. She also asked why (and how) I had managed to wait so long. I had been asking myself the same question. She also included an unsolicited opinion: "Stan's a problem." Tell me something I don't know, I thought. Still, Clarissa calling Einstein a problem sent a new wave of possibility through me.

From the window at the front of the bar, I saw Clarissa drive up in her brand-new Toyota Prius. Since she was still just partway through her MBA program, I assumed paying for it was something her father had helped her with, but I wasn't going to pry. She parked at a meter and paid with a credit card. It was getting dark. As she strode briskly under one of the bright streetlamps, her shadow shortened and pulled close to her, holding her tightly for a moment like a dancer, then pulled away again. I wanted her to turn around and walk back and forth under that streetlamp so I could watch this dance over and over.

She entered the bar. I stood as she approached the table.

"Easy on the chivalry there, cowboy."

"It's not chivalry. I have to go to the bathroom."

She didn't crack. "Nice to know you haven't changed."

Inside the men's room, there was a shiny metal urinal and one toilet in a stall. I chose to use the toilet, having always hated the sound of urine hitting sheet metal. Two varieties of condoms were for sale in a dispenser on the wall: Pleasure Studs and Safety Orange. Just for fun I turned the crank without putting any money in. A plain, unlubricated condom fell. I left it there. I washed my hands and returned to the table.

"The Tremendous Tater-Tot Tray," Clarissa said, handing the menu to me. "That sounds like my kind of appetizer."

"I don't recommend it. I think they reheat uneaten tots and serve them over and over until some unsuspecting drunkard—"

"Such as yourself?"

I held my hands up in an attempt to ward off any further judgment. "I know what you're implying. You're talking about how I am, like—"

"A problem drinker?"

"Let's skip the appetizers." I folded the menu and put it down.

"So why are we here, exactly?" she asked.

"I was hoping you'd help me get my robe back, that's all."

"The Pendleton?"

"How do you know it's a Pendleton?"

"Stan has it."

"Right, but how do you know?"

"I know a Pendleton when I see one."

"Well, I want it back. I should kill him for wearing it."

"Kill him? That's a joke. You're no killer. You'd think twice before canceling a stamp." She tapped her fingernails on the tabletop.

"I admit," I said, "that a certain amount of hostility can be endearing, even compelling. But at some point, it needs to be tempered with a little sympathy."

"Like the sympathy you showed for Pigeonhole when he almost died?"

"Let's focus on the robe. Any idea how I can get it back?"

"Here's the deal. Stan moved to Wisconsin. Sara is with him off and on. I can tell you exactly where."

"Where?"

"It's called the Chequamegon Pines. I have a brochure in my purse." She dug into her bag, reaching around in the bottom and pulling things out until, with the zest of a travel agent, she produced a brochure for the Chequamegon Pines Resort and Wellness Center. It looked like something from the 1990s—matte paper, kooky drawings, poor layouts, and horrible photography. It absolutely blew my mind that such a resort could even exist, other than maybe in a Christopher Guest or Noah Baumbach film. Still, the northwoods appeal of the place was undeniable. There were pictures of a pristine lake and cabins, photos of a well-tended organic garden, a traditional Finnish sauna, and a map with directions from Duluth, the Twin Cities, Madison, and Chicago.

"Looks interesting, no?" Clarissa asked.

"In a manner of speaking."

"You can keep that."

"Thanks," I said, folding up the brochure. "What's Einstein doing at a place like this, anyway?"

"Apparently, they hired him to spin records in the main lodge for events and on weekends when it's busy. For what it's worth, he says he loves it. He wants to move up there permanently, buy some land, live a simple life. Something like that. He put his store up for sale. No one's going to buy it, though, since it's really all about him. So he's just going to close up his brick-and-mortar. He'll keep Emcee Squared online, or so he says, as a tax write-off."

I will punish him, I thought. Teach him about pain. Pain and loss. Or just pain. "I think I'm going to pay him a little visit. I'd like to avoid Sara, though."

Clarissa looked incredulous after that last comment. "Then go during the week," she said. "Sara only visits on weekends."

I lost myself in my thoughts for a moment, my eyes focusing on the wall at the far end of the bar. Clarissa reached across the table and spread her fingers across my right triceps. I froze. She stared at me, and I stared back.

"Tell me, William. What hurts more," she asked, pulling her hand back, "losing Sara, losing her to someone like Stan, or losing your mind over it?"

I was shocked at her audacity, and more shocked at her use of the phrase "losing your mind." Was she serious? Had I actually lost my mind? And if so, was it that obvious? Outside, my mother fluttered across the street, up the sidewalk, and out of sight. The streetlights all went dark.

"That's weird," Clarissa said, pointing. "The dome light is on in my car." She searched her coat pocket, presumably for her keys. They weren't there. She stood and went outside.

I watched through the window. Clarissa opened driver's side door and found her keys on the seat. I left money on the table and met Clarissa at the curb.

"What happened?"

"I must have forgotten my keys."

"You got lucky," I said. "Anything stolen?"

"Someone took the robe."

"I can't win!"

"Only kidding. I don't have your robe. You'll have to get it from Stan."

"Think he'll give it back to me?"

"If you pretend you want it."

"What do you mean? I do want it."

"I mean, if you pretend that's all you want. Revenge is contagious. And it's not all it's cracked up to be." She stepped toward me and, out of the blue, kissed me on the cheek. "Just be careful."

As if none of the preceding had happened, she got in her car and drove off. I went back into the bar alone and studied the brochure from front to back. Looked like about a four-hour drive. I could get there on a weekday evening, pick out a cabin for myself, get the lay of the land, and formulate a plan. I guess I could only hope he had the robe up there, but why wouldn't he? A nice, vintage, plaid robe would be right at home at a lodge like that. He probably wore it while dee-jaying. But in any case, I knew Clarissa was right. The robe wasn't all I wanted.

CHAPTER 23

THE NEXT DAY I got an email from Caroline saying she would send the rest of the money she owed me, just over $7,000 at that point. All that week I waited for the check to come in the mail. On Saturday, instead of a check in my mailbox, I found an assortment of demanding letters from collection agencies and, oddly, an issue of *Rolling Stone,* a magazine to which I did not subscribe.

To the best of my ability, I ignored the Taylor Swift cover photo and opened the issue. Astonishment beyond all reckoning washed over me when I saw, on the very first page, a photo of Pigeonhole posed in a gilded wheelchair set against a backdrop of puffy clouds with a digitally rendered halo above his head. He bore an Eddie Van Halen model electric guitar across his shoulders like a cross. A crown of barbed wire in luminous gold was nestled into his thicket of dark, curly hair, now longer than ever. Below him, in Gothic lettering, were the words: "He Is Risen: The Advent of Pigeonhole."

I turned to the article. Pigeonhole was pictured in a two-page spread, flanked by five other guitar-wielding metalheads, several also in wheelchairs. The subtitle of the article was "A Rolling Christian Metal Band Gathers No Moss." I couldn't believe it was real. I went back upstairs with the magazine and scoured the article for any mention of the accident. A passage read:

RS: When did you hit rock bottom?

PH: Well, this crazy artist dude moves in next door to me, right? He seems to be a pretty much, you know, non-metal-type guy. I won't get into the details of how everything got started. Mainly because I can't remember them. But what I do remember is that after jumping down the stairs and nearly killing myself, I experienced what every near-death-experience survivor lives to tell about: the light. I witnessed this super-intense, IMAX-caliber white light. Then, suddenly, a vintage 1966 Stratocaster appeared before my eyes. I was in the house of Jimi. He told me it wasn't my time yet. I remember this part vividly. He pointed right at me and said, "You still got a few licks left to learn, little devil-man." Then everything turned into a purple haze, and I woke up in the hospital. All thanks to the fact that my neighbor, this artist dude, had burst into my apartment and thrown my cardboard Eddie Van Halen down the stairs.

RS: So you jumped down after it?

PH: It seemed like a good idea at the time. But that's when everything changed for the better. I guess what I'm saying is, along with my back, the viscous (sic) cycle was broken. I hit rock bottom when I hit those stairs. I ended up in rehab in every conceivable way, and because of that fall, I was reborn, so to speak, in the image of Jesus.

RS: So you're comparing yourself to Jesus?

PH: That was taken out of context.

RS: No, it wasn't.

PH: Well, what I'm saying is that Jesus died and was reborn so we could all copy him.

RS: You're saying we should all copy Jesus?

PH: It's not as easy as it sounds. Anyway, I'd like to do something nice for that dude someday.

RS: Who, Jesus?

PH: No, the artist dude. I bet he still has my cardboard cut-out of Eddie, too. I'd like to get that back. He was like the brother I never had.

RS: Who, the artist?

PH: No, the cardboard Eddie. Are you sure you're a reporter?

I went online to verify all of this. Pigeonhole's website stated he was about to embark on a nationwide tour, but, amazingly, he was still without a record deal. His music was all home recorded and released digitally. There was, in fact, no need for a record deal. Spotify, YouTube, Tidal, and Instagram were flooded with his music. He had short guitar tutorials on TikTok, along with glimpses into his physical therapy and long-winded, soulful prayers. How could all of this have happened in such a short time?

A lump formed in my throat as I watched one of Pigeonhole's rehab videos on my laptop. He was attempting, and failing, to walk unassisted. I closed the browser. I needed to go outside for some air. I grabbed the magazine to reassure myself that I wasn't hallucinating. On my way down the stairs, I ran into Vernon, who was ambling his way up, looking a little uncertain about his prospects for actually making it all the way up the stairs.

"Vernon." I held up the magazine. "Look what someone sent to me."

"I received a copy as well." He stopped to catch his breath.

"I can't believe it. I never thought this would happen in a million years."

Vernon took off his fedora and held it above his head. "I will offer you some advice, if I may."

I was not prepared for one of Vernon's extemporaneous therapy sessions.

"If you are to commit to your ideals, as I have, life can be very difficult at times. Humans are at the mercy of time and space." He moved his hat along like a hovering spaceship. "Don't let the horizon call out to you, William. The horizon is a liar. It doesn't even exist. You can't go there. You can only be here, where you are right now. It's always right here and right now." He put his hat back on. He clasped his hands behind his back and continued up the stairs, casually whistling. Before he reached the top of the stairwell, he stopped and turned. "Would you care to join me for dinner?"

I was out of food and still waiting for Caroline's next check, so I skipped the fresh air and followed him up to his apartment. It had been a while since I'd been in there, and I'd forgotten how big and airy it was. Freshly painted white walls enveloped five tall windows across the length of the apartment. He had replaced his old, junky couch and chairs with vintage bamboo patio furniture, including a glass-top table and a giant umbrella, open and tilted toward the windows. I sat at the table. Above me on the underside of the open umbrella was what appeared to be a screen print of Charles Manson's face.

"Not bad, eh?"

"Is this your work?"

"Of course," Vernon said. "I don't collect art."

"The image surprised me, that's for sure."

"All art should always be a surprise. Totally unexpected, and not always in a good way. Like a train wreck, but with as few casualties as possible."

I had never considered the act of looking at art as an orchestrated train wreck, but considering the absurd exigencies of the art world, it seemed appropriate. "Seems like something you'd want to avoid if possible."

"That's the point. You can't avoid a train wreck by choice. It either happens, or it doesn't. Kind of like falling in love. There's nothing you can do."

"Tell me about it," I said.

"Maybe I will."

"I'm all ears."

"Well, there's love, and there's its opposite: marriage."

"Ouch." I wasn't going to argue with him about that. "My mother never married, you know."

"A wise woman. She did, however, have children. Or a child, at least."

"Yes, she did. And I'm an only child." On the table sat a Warhol monograph. I opened it and was met, unsurprisingly, with the image of a can of tomato soup.

"A showman if there ever was one," Vernon said. "Warhol always reminded me of Lee Iacocca. Two geniuses of smoke-and-mirrors. We could all learn from them." He chose a bottle of wine from the shelf above the sink and tucked it under his arm.

"You think I should work at being a more of a showman?"

"You haven't made much progress on that front, I'll say that much. But that's because—and this may come as a surprise to you—you're afraid to."

I closed the book. Vernon started working a corkscrew into the bottle.

"Can we change the subject?" I asked.

"Sure." He handed me a glass.

"I'm going on a trip."

"Where?"

"To northern Wisconsin. I need to get my robe back. And I have some unfinished business with someone."

"Spoken like a true showman. When are you going?"

"Soon."

"I might have some information for you." He sat down. "There has been an unusually high number of UFO sightings in northern Wisconsin lately. Lots of buzz in the online forums. I was thinking of heading up there myself."

Jesus, I thought. All I need is a bunch of UFO true believers taking over the lodge and wrecking my plan. "I'm going to a place called the Chequamegon Pines Resort. Something like that. Einstein works there now."

"I've heard of that place. Lots of professors go there. Hippy-dippy ones, anyway."

Vernon popped back up, went to the kitchen, and peered into the refrigerator. "It seems the cupboard is bare." He closed the fridge. "I guess we're going out. On me. There's a new Laotian place in Dinkytown. You game?"

"I've heard good things," I said, which was a lie. I had hardly spoken to anyone in months, let alone about a new Laotian restaurant. Though I would have been game in any case.

"I want to show you something first," he said.

Vernon pulled the blinds and turned off the track lights. There was an old slide projector set up on the coffee table, facing the living room wall. He switched it on and began clicking through a series of images of UFOs—most of them of the distant "flying saucer" variety. In between these images were Vernon's portraits of the people who had taken the photos years earlier. Over several years, Vernon told me, he had traveled to photograph and hear the stories of these people. One person was clearly dying from cancer. Another was a church pastor. Another a retired car mechanic. It went on and on. The photos Vernon had taken were washed-out, over-exposed, and haunting. He also photographed the sites where people claimed to have seen the ships. Most appeared to be out West, maybe Montana, Idaho, Oregon, Utah. One had a sign from Harrison, Nebraska. Vernon was silent as he clicked through the final images. When he got to the last slide, he turned off the projector and walked over to the door.

"Let's go."

Chapter 24

CAN I STILL consider myself William's mother? I'm not so sure. He hardly even looks at me anymore. It seems as though he's trying to will me away. If that's true, it would be hard to blame him. But I can't be sure how he feels. He never speaks to me, and I can't hear anyway. And although I can paint, I'm no longer able to write. The words simply won't come. Believe me, I've tried. My writing ends up looking like shards of broken glass. Unreadable. Even if I could write to William, what on earth could I possibly say? It's a paintbrush that belongs in my hand, not a pen. This was as true when I was alive as it is now that I'm dead. Yet at this point I don't feel William wants to hear from me in any case.

I find myself standing outside William's apartment building. He is right in front of me, talking with the man from upstairs. This man is looking in my direction, and I wonder if he can see me. I suspect not. Either that, or he has the best poker face I've ever seen. William, for his part, isn't looking in my direction. He's got his phone out and is framing a picture of a pigeon sitting atop a recycling bin. Maybe he's capturing material for a painting. Maybe he's just curious how the bird will react. If it's for a painting, I'll find out soon enough.

The two move off down Cedar Avenue. I don't follow them. I head the other direction, toward the Mississippi River. I walk out onto the water and meander the entire way to downtown St. Paul. From there, I head through the West Side and into West St. Paul, where our house once stood. The house was a cookie-cutter '70s split-level rush job, perfect for something built on a drained swamp. Who knew that a cookie cutter could become a deadly weapon? From the outside, it appeared benign enough at the time—a two-car garage facing the street, a basketball hoop installed at nonregulation height, a central air unit attached at the side like a medical device. Migrating birds seemed to know a swamp had once been there, flying back and forth in formation in the spring and fall as if to say we did not belong there. They were right.

A new house has since been built in place of ours. But I can still hear the flames licking the walls, can still feel the rumble of the roof collapsing. It's as if the house never truly stopped burning. It's twilight now, and I can see the family who lives here sitting down to dinner. I wonder if they have any idea where they are living, what they are living in the shadow of. Maybe it wouldn't matter to them. And maybe it shouldn't. Time marches on, and we can't expect to bear witness to every single moment of human suffering that may have occurred in our midst. We forge ahead. Or most of us do.

My artwork was meant to bear witness to human suffering, but what it really did was give me an excuse suffer more myself. That's not something I miss. Working on William's paintings is a far more fertile pursuit. While I used to work on my own paintings obsessively, I contribute to William's only in fits and starts—sometimes feverishly, sometimes apprehensively, sometimes not at all. Helping him with his paintings is really the only pleasure I have left in this world.

And while it is a pleasure, I help him less than he thinks. There's more of him in his work than there is of me. He does things I never would have thought to try, could never hope to execute on my own. Maybe he feels the same way about my help, but I suspect he's giving me too much credit. I don't want him to misunderstand my motives. I wish I could just speak to him, talk with him about the work directly, and that he could hear me, as if I were still alive, as if none of this had ever happened. But that isn't how this works, whatever this is. Everything remains in that rear-view mirror.

But even if I could speak, what would I say? I couldn't just sit down and start prattling on about his paintings or my efforts to work on them. There would be too many other things that would need to be said. First and foremost: Why did I do what I did? It wouldn't matter if I could actually put it into words. The only person who would ever understand is a person who is about to strike their own fateful match. William is not like that, thank goodness. And whether I'm watching him work, watching him sleeping alone at night, or watching him watch me, there is a veil between us, one that I suspect will be there forever.

When he's with another person, I try to keep my distance, at least for the most part. I watch them from as far away as I can, or if that's still too close, I'll wander off on my own for a while. Instinctively, I know when to return. Call it a mother's intuition. But with all the wandering he's been doing lately, I'm surprised I've been able to keep track of him. A mother keeping tabs on her child is another form of intuition, I suppose, though I never had a good sense of direction in the living world. Now I do. Call it the intuition of the dead.

Chapter 25

I HAD BEEN working steadily on both the painting of my mother and the one of Sara. Neither was close to finished, and both were causing me tremendous grief. Finally, the check from Caroline came. A bit less than promised, but it was enough. There was no longer a reason to wait. It was time for me to pay a visit to the Chequamegon-Nicolet National Forest, find Einstein, and, at the very, very least, get my robe back.

I methodically packed my car for the trip. I packed a single change of clothes, toiletries, my travel easel, the minimum number of tubes of paint I could work with, two small blank canvases, and, for good measure, Pigeonhole's slingshot. I had checked the resort's website for vacancies, and it turned out they had so few bookings for that week that I could just show up without a reservation. I wasn't sure if Einstein might have access to the registrations, and I didn't want to tip my hand.

I hit the road first thing on a Tuesday morning. I took the route suggested in the resort's brochure: east on Highway 8, northeast on US Highway 63 through Spooner, Hayward, and Drummond. From there, I headed south on a narrow, winding stretch of road that led into a shallow valley dotted with tiny lakes. As my car struggled to climb a steep grade, I approached an expanse of tall grass with stands of shimmering cottonwoods beyond. At a crossroads, a painted wooden sign pointing to the left read "Chequamegon Pines Resort." I turned. The road narrowed further, twisting as it took me through blind turns between chains of modest lakes and into seemingly dead-end ravines, only to twist out again, the road mimicking the path of a darting northwoods deer. So lacking in straight passages was this terrain that I spent nearly an hour traveling just twenty miles. As I made my way, the nearby small towns—Cable, Mellen, Clam Lake—advertised themselves on hand-painted billboards, most in weathered disrepair.

The sun began its descent as deer emerged from the trees and onto the road, their eyes glowing in the light of my car's headlights. After a long bend in the road, I came to a lodge with several cabins surrounding it. A sign read "You Made It!"

I pulled my car into the gravel lot and stopped under a towering oak. Through the lodge windows, I could see a small café with two men milling around in an orderly kitchen. I entered and sat down at the counter.

The shorter of the two men approached. "Driving give you an appetite, son?" I nodded. "Well, you got here in the nick of time. We were just about to close the kitchen. But listen, I can have Brint here whip you up a special plate. My name's Dean." He pointed to the other man with a tilt of his head. "This here's my partner, Brint."

"Howdy," Brint said. I couldn't place their accents, but they were clearly not from Wisconsin or anywhere even close.

"Something to drink?" Dean set his thumbs under the strings of his apron.

"Diet Coke?"

"Well, where I come from—that's Texas if you couldn't tell—it's regular Coke or nothing. But here at The Pines we only have organic soda. Pure cane sugar. Don't worry, it won't kill you." He set a bottle in front of me. "So, what brings you up this way?"

I pictured my robe and imagined myself wearing it to the TimeWarp in a moment of ill-found triumph. "I'd say I'm kind of on a mission."

"A mission! Son, there's only two kinds of missions, business or pleasure. Which kind you on?"

"Maybe both?"

"Well, if The Pines ain't the place to do it all. In fact, Brint and I met right here at the resort during a cubic zirconium convention years back." He glanced at Brint, then back at me. "It was industrial uses, son, not jewelry. I took one look at Brint in his blue ultra-suede sport coat and white rattlesnake boots, and I had palpitations of historic proportions. We knew we were meant for each other when we both wanted to go deer hunting as our first date. How's your soda?"

I nodded. I glanced at a flyer taped to the wall by the door. Pigeonhole was playing the nearby Bayfield Blues Festival that weekend. I shuddered to think of the Wisconsin mullet crowd crawling out of the woods just to hear him play.

"Brint, get this man a venison steak and some wild rice. You like venison, son?"

I blinked and checked the clock behind the cash register.

"Now picture this. Me and Brint were huddled behind a tall white pine." He squatted a bit for effect. "All of a sudden I hear some scratchin' on the ground, and I lean around the tree trunk to see what it was. That's when I caught the eighth point of an eight-point buck right across my left ear. Sheared it clean off like a shoemaker's jig."

"What's a shoemaker's jig?"

"Right. But then, when the deer smelled blood, he leaped over a thorn bush and puffed away like an old fire-breathin' dragon. I saw my ear on the ground and fainted like a daisy in December. But Brint kept his cool. He picked up my little van Gogh and put it in his pocket. Then he picked me up and carried me back to the lodge. He put the ear on ice and tried to get us to Duluth to get it sewed back on, but it weren't no use. I got it in a jar in back. You reckon you want to see the ear, son?"

I stared blankly in no particular direction. Dean signaled Brint, who set a plate of wild rice in front of me. It had morels, ramps, and cranberries, all locally sourced, I imagined. "Steak ready in a minute. Be right back," Dean said. He walked through the kitchen, presumably to get the ear.

"We lived together in Oklahoma City for years," he shouted from the back room. "Then we came back here last year for our anniversary and decided to buy the lodge, and the rest is history." He returned empty-handed. Only then did I see the stump where his ear once was. "Never mind the ear now," he said. "This man needs to eat!"

Once I finished the meal, Dean suggested we take my car from the lodge to the resort's oldest cabin, which was several hundred yards away. I agreed, as it was now completely dark. From the passenger seat, Dean directed me down a rutted dirt trail to the ancient cabin, isolated in the woods. A rocking chair sat on a small porch facing the lake. Pine trees and narrow aspens surrounded the cabin so densely they blocked all light from the lodge. The moon and its reflection off the lake provided the only illumination.

"We call this cabin Old Dorothy," he said. "She was the original owner a hundred years ago. We don't usually rent her out, but you seem like the right type." Dean put the key in the lock and opened the door. He reached in and switched on the porch light. "How long you plan to stay?" he asked. "It's sixty-five a night, but you get a discount if you stay the week."

"Just one night."

He nodded and said I could pay the next morning. He pulled a small flashlight from his pocket and headed back through the dark woods on foot.

The cabin—a bargain at $65 a night—had one large room, a tiny kitchen tucked in the corner, a fieldstone fireplace in the opposite corner, and a large full bathroom in back. I put all my things on the bed and emptied my pockets, which had filled up on the trip to a considerable extent: my old iPod, earbuds, a piece of gum, one Wisconsin lottery scratch game (which was a loser but still graphically interesting), two camera batteries that turned out to be the wrong kind for my mother's old film camera, $3.15 in coins from buying snacks and soda here and there, and a book of matches that I picked up at a gas station in Drummond. I was glad about the matches because I needed them to get the fireplace going. There was plenty of wood and enough kindling, and I used the lottery ticket to get it all started.

As the fire caught, I moved out to the front porch and sat in the old rocking chair. I listened to the chair runners creak, the blades dulled by the years, smooth as old wagon wheels, the sound a fitting rhythm beneath the cottonwoods rustling in the breeze. A black spider crawled across the railing toward me. The spider, as if she had noticed me at the same moment I noticed her, dropped stealthily off the railing onto the shadowy porch floor. A few seconds later she sprinted right toward my chair. I stopped rocking. When she was within a few feet of me, she halted, then began to stop and start, moving in minuscule spurts no more than half an inch at a time and in no particular direction. I slowly raised my right foot and brought it down flat and hard onto the floor right next to her. The porch shook, and the sound echoed across the lake. The spider flew off the side of the porch and was gone.

That was when my mother appeared, sitting on the railing where the spider had been. She took a breath, stood, and pulled at the pleats of her tattered dress. Ash fell at her feet as she took a step toward the cabin door. As if probing for a heartbeat, she pressed her hand against the torso of the door. After a moment, she passed right through the door and went inside. I opened the door and followed.

The objects on the bed interested her. First, she picked up her old camera and framed a picture of the fireplace through the viewfinder. Setting the camera down in favor of the coins, she examined at each one, both heads and tails. She put one in her mouth and bit down. Finally, she eyed the matchbook. This unsettled me, and I retreated to the far wall of the kitchen, watching my mother from there. She held the matchbook and moved to touch the log mantle and the mortar between the stones of the chimney, acting as if this cabin were a distant memory. The docile fire in the fireplace made her smile the way a wizard might smile at an amateur magician's sleight of hand. She picked up the iron poker and stabbed at the logs, muttering something under her breath. She grew frustrated with the poker and instead used her hands. The light penetrated her hair, reaching her scalp, highlighting the ashen tangles. Then, without warning, just like always, my mother disappeared.

I was exhausted. I went into the bathroom and closed the door. I drew hot water into the tub. As it filled, I undressed and sat down in the tub, splashing water onto my face and over my head. I leaned back to rest. After a time, I began dozing a little. The sound of the cabin door slamming startled me awake. I drained the tub and opened the bathroom door.

I went out to my car to get my travel easel and paints. Once I had everything set up, I spread paint on my palette and stared at the blank canvas in front of me. The fire seemed to be picking up steam, though I had not added any more wood. The room was glowing orange. It was then I realized I forgot to bring my portable work lights. Even with the overhead light on, the fire roaring, and the moonlight through the window, I couldn't see the colors I was trying to work with. I set my brush down and picked up my mother's old Pentax film camera. I photographed the inside of the cabin, the log walls, the fieldstones, the wool blanket, and the wrought iron bed. I advanced the film one last time and set the camera on the mantle, lens facing out. I lay down on the bed. Everything that had been swimming circles in my head fell away, and sleep came over me.

Chapter 26

WHEN I AWOKE, I rose from the bed and stood in my bare feet. A thin layer of ash covered the floorboards. The metal guard in front of the fireplace had tipped forward. I set it back up and checked the flue. It had fallen closed. Perhaps a gust of wind caused this, but I believed my mother had done it. I looked around for any other signs of her presence overnight.

There on the easel was a finished painting of a woman holding the receiver of an old dial telephone to her ear. Her mouth was closed; she appeared to be just listening. The woman in the painting looked a bit like my mother, but it wasn't exactly a self-portrait. But she sat the same way, held her fingers around the receiver in the same way. I took the painting off the easel and put it on the mantle. It looked so good there I decided I would leave it behind.

I picked up the camera and checked the shutter. It had been tripped, meaning a picture had been taken overnight. The film would need to be developed before I could see what it was, if anything, beyond the cabin interior. Would I end up with a photograph of my mother? I bagged the camera and got everything else packed into my car. I wanted to be ready to leave this place in a hurry if need be.

My phone buzzed. It was a text from Vernon. It read:

Dear William,

You are to meet me this evening in Cornuco-pia, Wisconsin, at the corner of Superior and Elm, in front of the post office, at precisely six o'clock. I'll have more info for you at that time. Don't be late, and don't do anything you'll regret. Unless you'll regret not doing it more, of course.

Until then,
Vernon

I wasn't sure I'd still be in Wisconsin by that time, and I didn't reply. With my car packed up, I checked the cabin one last time. I locked the door and walked back to the lodge. It was farther back through the woods than I remembered. The woods were so thick and dark it didn't look all that different from how it had appeared the night before.

When I entered the lodge, Dean was at the counter.

"Sleep well, I hope?"

I realized I had. "Very well. But the chimney flue fell closed. Was it windy last night?"

"Come again?"

"Last night. Was there a lot of wind?"

"Well, son, this is an unpredictable area weatherwise, be-ing so close to Superior and all. It might have been."

I handed him my key and credit card. Dean processed the charge. I asked him if I could wander the grounds for a while and look around. I didn't mention who I was looking for or why. "Of course. The resort's all yours for the rest of the day.

Gonna be fairly warm. You could even take a dip in the lake if you want. Just watch out for bears."

"Bears?"

"Kidding! Sort of. Anyway, it would be great if you could clear out of the cabin so we can send the maid in. We got this new guy by the name of Einstein. He doesn't like to get behind schedule."

"Einstein?" I played dumb. I couldn't believe his job involved cleaning cabins.

"Not quite like the one you're thinking about. This is a guy up from Minneapolis. He spins records at our events, but we've got him cleaning cabins when it's slow. I'd avoid him if I were you. He's kind of, uh, off, if you catch my drift." He tapped his finger to his temple. "You catch my drift?"

"Off? You mean, like, a lunatic?"

"That's it, son. A lunatic! We give him a free cabin way up on the other side of the property. Don't see hide nor hair, for the most part. He floats his ass around the lake on an inner tube all morning, then cleans cabins in the afternoon. At night he picks on an old guitar and plays records by himself. No motivation whatsoever. Motivation is important, son."

"I couldn't agree more."

"On weekends he has a visitor up from the Cities. His girlfriend, I suspect."

"Only on weekends?" I asked, with maybe a bit too much emphasis on "only."

Brint gave me a curious stare. "That's right, son. Maybe she works weekdays. Who knows?"

I did. And Sara was the last person I wanted to encounter up here. I realized just then that I had never asked Clarissa to keep this trip to herself. Somehow I trusted she would.

"I think I'll head down to the lake," I said. "By the way, I keep a slingshot in my car for fun. Do you mind if I, you know, take a few shots at some tree branches and whatnot?"

"Sure. Pays to stay in practice." He rubbed the spot where his ear had been. "Here's your receipt. Come again, I hope."

I walked back to my car and opened the rear hatch. I dug underneath my art supplies for the slingshot. I grabbed some marbles I had stashed in a pouch and stuffed them into my pocket. I wrapped the slingshot in a beach towel, tucked it under my arm, and cut across the property toward the lake. Dean and Brint waved at me through the kitchen window.

Near the shore, I noticed an old ice fishing house. It was unlocked, and I entered. A small, open window faced the lake. I scanned the water. Near an overhanging oak tree, I spotted a lone man floating on an inner tube. The shock of white hair, the impossibly skinny torso, the pipe-cleaner limbs: Clearly, it was Einstein. An old wooden dock jutted into the water, and hanging from a post on the dock was my Pendleton robe. I could not believe this asshole was making things so easy. I estimated the distance and running time back to my car. I convinced myself I could do this, though I wasn't sure if it would be worth it.

I mounted the slingshot on my left arm, exited the icehouse, and walked out onto the dock. Einstein had rigged up an old record player at the end of the dock with a car battery. It was playing something by Toto. It wasn't "Africa," but I wasn't sure of the track. I could hear the distinctive guitar tones of Steve Lukather, something Pigeonhole had played over and over when he wasn't drowning in his own shredding. I shivered when I saw the belt of my robe dangling down just far enough to grace the water's surface. I knew I could simply snatch the robe and run, but I was no longer fooling myself. I wasn't there for the robe. I raised the slingshot and pulled a steel marble from my pocket. Einstein was still floating, oblivious. The song ended, and the next one started. Again, not "Africa," but that was fine with me. I lifted the slingshot, put the marble into the pouch, and aimed it directly at Einstein. In the light breeze, he was rotating nearly imperceptibly counterclockwise. I planned to go for the groin. I was patient. His yellow swimming trunks made things a bit easier. I held my breath and released the projectile. A second later Einstein jumped like a bullfrog stung by a hornet.

"Motherfucker!" He spotted me. He thrashed through the water, churning back toward the dock with giant windmill arm strokes.

I plucked my robe from the pole. All I needed to do was run away, get to my car, and drive off. Instead, in a moment of temporary insanity, I took off my shoes, socks, pants, and T-shirt, and dove into the water. I paddled toward Einstein, slowly, saving my strength. As I approached, he wiped snot from his nose and shrieked, "You fucking cock!" He came at me, knifing forward with both arms. I backstroked away, but he grabbed my ankle and pulled me underwater. From behind, he bear-hugged me, then attempted to strangle me. I elbowed him until he let go, but a second later he latched on again and pulled me under. Clawing at him as I desperately struggled to reach the surface, I inadvertently pulled his hair. Something let loose in my hands. There, right in front of my eyes, brightly lit in the clear, cold spring water, was Einstein's hairpiece. It was, I have to admit, a rather impressive specimen. If Clarissa hadn't told me, I would never have known. Clutching the rug, I swam back to the dock and climbed out.

I held the hairpiece above my head. Einstein was draped atop his inner tube, giving me the finger over and over like an animated GIF. He had a bit less hair loss than I, and I was stung by a pinprick of jealousy. I took another look at the robe, and its presence repulsed me. Had I really come up here for this? Of course not. I threw his hair into the lake, plucked the robe off the pole, and tossed that in, too. Then I kicked the record player, and the music abruptly stopped. Mission accomplished. With my shoes, clothes, and the slingshot all bundled under my arm, I ran back toward my car. Dean and Brint, still looking out the window, both gave me a thumbs-up.

I tossed everything into the backseat and jumped behind the wheel, soaking wet and barefoot. The engine turned but failed to start. I gripped the wheel with enough force to snap a paintbrush, something I had done many times. Why was I thinking about painting at a time like this? But when wasn't I thinking about it? I kept my eye out for any sign of Einstein. I tried the ignition again, and this time the engine caught. I threw the transmission into reverse, turned the car around, slammed it into drive, and floored it. A minute later I was on the road heading back to the highway. No one followed.

At that moment I realized I had completely lost control and no longer knew what I was doing. I also realized that what had just transpired was something I would surely come to regret.

CHAPTER 27

AS A PRECOCIOUS girl and later as a teenager, I was far ahead of the other girls in most respects. I'm not sure "precocious" is the right word, because I was ignorant of a great many things my peers seemed to know instinctively—in particular things about boys and love and kissing and dating and all that—but I can't think of a better word. "Mature" isn't right either, though I seemed to have an adult's sense of purpose behind my thoughts and actions. For starters, I didn't think of school as the insufferable burden most of my childhood friends did. I felt at home in school, as if I had specifically chosen it from among many other possible paths. But of course no one does that. We all simply end up in school, just as we end up in diapers before that or end up in the womb before that. I'm not sure why I felt as if it were a choice I had made. Maybe I was able to envision choices other children could not, choices that were only in my head, like being buried alive, or getting lost in the woods for a year, or living on a foreign cargo ship with dozens of crewmen but no other children. These kinds of thoughts came to me long before I ever had true hallucinations or heard voices that weren't really there. But there was an inkling of things to come: Life as it appeared on the surface was far from all there was to behold.

One day, when I was fourteen or fifteen, I looked out my bedroom window, and there on the roof of the house next door was a man standing, staring right at me. He was not the owner of the house. I had never seen him before. I pulled the curtains closed. I waited for what seemed like ten minutes but was probably just thirty seconds. When I opened the curtains again, he was still there. I screamed, and my mother came rushing in. She couldn't see the man. This was my first ever hallucination. My mother scolded me, calling me crazy.

There were other reasons to avoid my mother, but after that I wanted nothing to do with her. I remember there was an apple orchard in the town where I grew up. It wasn't on a busy street, so that meant if you were driving on that street, you either lived on it or were going to the orchard. As soon as I got my driver's license, that is where I spent most of my time driving, one mile up, U-turn in the orchard parking lot, one mile back. Repeat. I drove for fun, for something to do, to avoid my mother, and for other reasons. To visit Becky, for example.

Becky was then—and maybe still is, I don't know—someone I would have liked to get to know, but never really did. Becky was my age, but a grade ahead of me. She was short with pale skin, long black hair, and eyes like cherries. I swear they were dark red. She never seemed to blink, as if she were afraid to miss something in the split second it takes to lower the eyelids and raise them again. I wondered if she slept with her eyes open. Maybe I wondered too much. Because Becky wasn't real. She was my second hallucination. There would be many more.

Years later, when William entered grade school, I found myself regularly hospitalized for my condition. With William staying at my mother's, or my mother staying at our house until my return, the hospital staff knew they could keep me there for as long as they felt it necessary. My memory of most visits is a blur, but there are times when I recall receiving shock treatments. I remember the shocks the way a nail might remember being pounded by a hammer.

I've stayed out of that particular hospital, Divine Redeemer, since my death. I've no desire to see any of those rooms or people again. But I do visit the hospital grounds. People who die at the side of the road often get a shrine to honor their passing. But people who die at, or because of, or in spite of hospitals have no such shrine. It's as if hospitals play no part in death, but that's nonsense. People pass these roadside shrines and wonder who it was, how it happened, when it occurred. Though it's all obvious: Someone you didn't know and didn't love got hit by a car and died. But few do this with hospitals. Either way, there are no shrines to the dead when the death is self-inflicted. There are no memorial wreaths in suburban homes when lives end there.

I remember once buttering a piece of white bread for William when he was very young, the restaurant butter knife probably appearing to him as large as a mortar trowel, the bread so white it looked like vellum, a story unwritten. William seemed so free from concern when I handed him that slice of bread. Nothing yet to lose at that age, or so you think. But there is always a knife in wait—to be fallen upon, or thrust inward, or at least flashed quickly to anyone looking, then put back in its sheath until such time as it needs to be used. And every knife knows its time.

CHAPTER 28

IT DIDN'T HAVE to be this way. Instead of going through with it, my mother could have just as easily tripped on her way down the stairs and knocked herself out or passed out from the pills, or I could have simply refused to go to my grandmother's house that day. She could have met the right psychiatrist or gotten on a better prescription. Or a worse one. Or it could have rained that day, causing her to curl up in a ball under the covers to wait it out. Or the car could have broken down. Or anything. Anything except what happened. To me, it wasn't inevitable, any more than tumbling down a mountain is inevitable. You have to climb it first.

But none of that happened. What happened, happened. So why would I let myself get caught up in thoughts that have no bearing on reality, no useful purpose whatsoever? Why would I continue to listen to some of the same music we listened to in that basement all those years ago? Why would I stare into the flame of a burning candle as if it were some kind of portal or oracle?

One of the earliest memories I have of her, aside from her painting in her basement studio, was of her dressing me as a vampire for Halloween. I was probably five, maybe four. It was the first time I had ever worn any kind of makeup. I remember looking into the mirror in our bathroom after she had applied a ghoulish white base, fake blood around my lips, and dark pencil to accentuate my eyebrows. I was shocked that it was me underneath that paint—shocked that I could become someone else on the outside, but still be myself on the inside, while somehow occupying an imaginary space between them both. I felt I was different, changed, and that I would somehow remain changed even when the makeup was removed.

When we were ready to trick-or-treat, we turned off all the lights in our house, locked the door, and walked up and down the streets of our neighborhood together. Of all things, she was dressed as a nurse. She sent me door to door, taking pictures the whole time and cackling a bit when I got scared at some of the spookier houses. I thought maybe it was some kind of test, but not a test that could be passed—only failed in various ways.

My Halloween bag was overflowing, and I asked my mother if we could stop. I wanted to go home and eat candy, listen to the Halloween record she had purchased for the occasion, and get out of the costume. I had had enough. I didn't know how to ask, so I just said, "Is Halloween over yet?" She removed her nurse's hat and said, "Halloween never ends, William. It just goes to sleep." Her use of the word sleep scared me in the strangest way.

When we got home, my mother began to remove the makeup from my face with a towelette, but I decided I wanted her to leave it on. I wanted to see if I would wake up the next day and still be a vampire, whether or not that was possible, or if I would die when the sun rose the next morning.

I said this to my mother, and she slapped me. I've never come up with a reasonable explanation for that. It was the only time I remember her ever hitting me. Maybe it was the way I asked it. Maybe it was the idea that I could, in fact, die—not from wearing vampire makeup, but for any reason at all. It might have meant something entirely different to her. I don't know. But she marched me into the bathroom and used Oil of Olay to remove the rest of makeup, or most of it anyway, and I have no memory of what happened after that.

Subsequent Halloweens with my mother went by without incident, and we never talked about the vampire costume again. But I always imagined her dressing up as a vampire on the day she died, putting on a cartoonish amount of makeup to heighten the drama or to allow herself, in some inexplicable way, to survive the unsurvivable.

CHAPTER 29

I DROVE STRAIGHT north, away from the lodge, toward Lake Superior. For the first 20 miles, I spent as much time looking in the rearview mirror as looking at the road ahead, but Einstein never appeared. I was officially on the lam. Once I got to the lake shore, I drove west for a few miles. After fifteen minutes or so, I made the final jaunt toward Siskiwit Bay and the tiny town of Cornucopia. I wasn't sure yet if I'd wait for Vernon, but I had no other plans. My mission, such as it was, had ended. All there was left to do was anticipate the fallout.

As I struggled to get out of my car in front of a small grocery store, I noticed some pain in my right leg when I tried to put weight on it. I limped into the store, and along with a bottle of ibuprofen, I bought a ham sandwich, a Diet Coke, and a bag of baby carrots. Sitting in the parking lot, I ate the sandwich and guzzled the Diet Coke, the windows rolled down, sunroof open, the slingshot visible in the front seat next to me. I wondered if I shouldn't ditch the slingshot somewhere. Isn't that how they do things in the movies? I rolled the slingshot back up in a towel. I wasn't sure what to do with it, so I plopped it back on the passenger seat.

I drove for a few blocks—meaning the entire length of the town—and pulled up in front of "Wisconsin's Northernmost

Post Office," which also appeared to be Wisconsin's smallest and dingiest post office. Vernon stood at the curb, suitcase in hand.

"Good afternoon, William," he said, stroking his beard. "You're early this time. The normal notion of time, that is, which is totally wrong."

"So what's the deal, Vernon?"

"The deal, William, is this: Tonight there will be an alien encounter at the coordinates listed on this piece of paper." He handed me a hand-drawn map with the words "Bark Bay Road, Past the Swamp" written across the top.

"These aren't coordinates."

"Give this to Carl Sagan and he would tell you otherwise. Such was his strength of vision, the power to grasp the infinite, to witness the infinitesimal. Billions and billions. A googol—a one with a hundred zeros after it. A googol plex—a one with a googol zeros after it. Huge. Big, big numbers."

"Okay, I'll try to make it."

"See you out there." Vernon pointed straight up, then walked off down Superior Street. I folded the map and stuffed it in my pocket. Vernon stopped and turned his head. "You might want to get rid of that weapon before tonight. Aliens don't appreciate projectiles."

When had he seen the slingshot? While I was in the store? Leave it to Vernon to follow me around the boondocks. I shivered as I thought of that steel marble launching across the water and striking Einstein in the scrotum. What I needed was a little more driving—enough to put some distance between me and my recent actions. So I drove west on Highway 13, toward Minnesota. I didn't want to go to Vernon's coordinates. I wanted to be at home, in my new robe. The one Einstein had never worn. After an hour or so, I took a break in a campground. Parked under a huge oak tree, I lay my head back and drifted off.

When I awoke, the sky across the eastern horizon had darkened into violet. The clouds to the west reflected a bright pink. I felt light as air and wondered if I was awake or asleep. I checked the seat next to me. The slingshot was still there. I unwrapped the towel. Inside was a message from Vernon.

> Dear William,
> Behind your many fine traits, a carelessness lurks. If you choose to miss this opportunity to witness history, I doubt you will receive another.
> Truly,
> Vernon

What the hell? This left me no choice. I turned back and headed east toward Vernon's coordinates. I was well off the main highway, and soon it would be dark. The hills and valleys were craggy, with exposed rock jutting out here and there. Farms and fences trailed off into wide-open valleys in one direction, the end-of-earth gravity of Lake Superior pulled from the other. Over a hill, I arrived at a spot where the road dropped sharply and came close to the edge of a deep gorge. Several communication towers stood a few miles to the south. The sun was setting. Gathering clouds to the north reminded me of the unpredictable weather Dean had mentioned. The landscape was disappearing into the coming darkness, and the stars had begun to fade in. The land flattened again, and the road straightened out as far ahead as I could see.

As I passed a rusted Quonset hut, my car's motor began to sputter and hesitate. I checked the gas gauge. More than half full. The oil pressure light came on, followed by a sound from the engine like a chainsaw. After a few seconds, I lost all power—the engine, lights, fan, everything. I let the car coast for a quarter mile on a slight downhill grade. I pulled to the side of the road as my car crept to a standstill. With my hands needlessly gripping the wheel, I sat for several minutes as the final traces of sun disappeared. I cranked the ignition key a few times. Nothing.

Not far up the road there was a billboard that read: "Wind—Powering the Future of Bayfield County." I read it over and over. There was a mock windmill projecting from the billboard with motorized blades spinning steadily in defiance of the still air. I got out of my car and slammed the door. I opened it again and pulled the hood release, then walked around to the front of the car and opened the hood.

The battery terminals were tight. Everything else looked fine, partly because it was dark, but mostly because I didn't know any better. I left the hood open and reached through the open passenger window for the slingshot. I still had a few marbles in my pocket. I took aim at the spinning propeller blades and tried to hit one—a moving target, but not exactly an unpredictable one. The first shot was a miss, as was the second. I kept taking shots until I was out of marbles. I managed a few hits. The cheap metal blades were hollow, and each hit echoed loudly across the landscape.

A few drops of rain fell. I searched the sky for clouds. It was completely clear. I approached the billboard and stood directly beneath it. Eight feet up the metal mast hung a ladder. I set the slingshot down, jumped up, and grasped the bottom rung. I pulled myself up—I had always been good at pull-ups—and began to climb. The ladder led to a platform running along the front of the sign. Its bright yellow background and buzzing lights overwhelmed me as I walked across the length of the sign. The spinning windmill blades guarded the other end where a second ladder led to the very top. In time with the rotation of blades, I ducked underneath, grabbed the second ladder, and climbed to the top. I stood atop the narrow edge of the sign, steadying myself. I gained my balance and took a step forward. Then another.

The sun had just set, and the pool of light around the billboard drowned out most of what there was to see. I looked straight down, expecting, or at least hoping, to see my mother wandering the ground beneath me, maybe working on my car or sitting in the passenger seat waiting for me. But there was no sign of her. Other than the headlights of a vehicle approaching in the distance, I was alone. The car was a mile away at least. I balanced on the top of the billboard and waited. A minute later, the car pulled up and stopped in front of the billboard. It was Vernon.

"These are not the designated coordinates!" he shouted.

"No?"

"No!" He pointed. "The exact spot is just over that ridge."

"How'd you find me?"

He got out of the car. "I heard loud clangs and came to investigate."

"I hit the windmill a few times with Pigeonhole's slingshot."

"Sound travels for miles around here. I had a weird feeling it was you."

Just then, as if to prove his point, the faintest sound came from the direction of the ridge—a distant howling of wind, though the air was as still as could be. From my position atop the billboard, I could see, far up the road, a pulsating cluster of lights. Soon came a sound that rose and fell in pitch, vaguely musical but barely audible above the buzzing of the billboard lights and the groan of the windmill's motor.

The object moved closer and slowly became a flurry of multicolored beams of light whirring just above the ground. Vernon picked up the slingshot.

"Never mind the coordinates," Vernon shouted. "This is it!"

The howling, ringing sound grew louder and began to take on a regular pattern. My spine stiffened, and my palms began to sweat. It did seem to be some type of craft, but it wasn't flying more than a few feet above the ground. Owing to the number, strength, and movement of the lights and the furious, bell-like projection of sound drowning out the buzzing billboard, it was unlike anything I had ever witnessed.

Depth perception failed me as the intense beams and spots of light compressed and expanded the distance between the craft and the billboard. In the surrounding darkness, I had no idea how big the craft was or how far away. I looked straight up to relieve my eyes from the stab of lights. As I did, I lost my balance briefly. I stepped back, then crouched down and straddled the sign to keep from falling.

The craft slowed as it approached. When it neared the billboard, I could see the shiny metal hull. It stopped right in the center of the road. A portal opened, and a puff of smoke was released. A lift gate descended carrying two seated figures.

"Hey, up there!" one of them yelled. "Don't be a jumper!"

It was Pigeonhole, his tour bus, and his band. The bus was equipped with external loudspeakers, which were blaring recordings of his instrumental compositions to the road in perfect time with a light show of glowing LED panels, clusters of bulbs, motorized spotlights, and fiber-optic curb feelers, all computer-controlled to pulsate to the rhythm of his music.

"I'm not going to jump, Pigeonhole!"

He rolled his chair off the lift and came closer to the sign. "How do you know my name?"

"The side of your bus says Pigeonhole in huge letters."

"Oh, yeah."

"Plus you're famous now."

"Oh, yeah."

"Plus I used to live right next door to you until you jumped down the stairs."

He did a triple take. "Dudeman! Is it literally you? Hey, you're not going to take a nasty plunge off that sign, are you?"

"I told you, I'm not jumping. My car died. I thought I was stranded."

"Stranded? Why not truck out of here with us? There's plenty of room left on the bus!" Pigeonhole leaned toward his bandmate and said, "Hey, that totally rhymed. Can you remember that for later?" His bandmate nodded, and Pigeonhole turned back to me. "We're heading south from the Bayfield Blues Fest. Where we rocked. I have an appointment at the Mayo Clinic for some tests tomorrow, but we can drop you off on the way. Deal?"

I would have to leave my car behind. It appeared so small and feeble from so far above, especially compared to Pigeonhole's giant tour bus. Not a great loss, but not inconsequential.

"Okay," I said, "on one condition."

"What?"

"Can you turn off the music?"

"Temporary deal." He signaled the driver, and the music was cut.

I climbed down.

Vernon approached us, carrying the slingshot.

"Wow, Vernon, how'd you get my Wrist Rocket?" Pigeonhole asked. "I never thought I'd see that thing again."

Vernon handed it to Pigeonhole. He cradled it like it was a relic from another century. "This belonged to my dad," Pigeonhole said, solemnly. "Who I only met once. Also, why are you here?"

Vernon looked at me as if I would know what to say, then pointed up the road and asked, "Would you like to witness history, or—?"

"I think I'm going to take a raincheck," I said.

"Suit yourself," Vernon said. "I'm going back to the exact coordinates. If you miss anything, I'll let you know. Unless, of course, I get abducted again."

Vernon said goodbye, got into his car, and drove off toward the ridge.

"What was that all about?" Pigeonhole asked.

"Aliens," I said.

"It's never aliens," he said.

"Until it's aliens," I said.

"Dude, you're so right."

Pigeonhole put the Wrist Rocket onto his forearm. I searched the ground for a pebble, picked one up, and handed it to him. He took a shot at the billboard. "I'm way out of practice."

As I went to my car to get my things, he kept picking up stones and firing at the billboard, every single shot a miss.

CHAPTER 30

WITH NO HOPE of ever seeing my car again, I cleaned it out and left it for dead. By this time, Pigeonhole was back on the bus. I climbed aboard. The interior was made to look like the belly of a whale. Pink carpeting everywhere, floor to ceiling, and white ribs down the length of the interior. I sat at a table near the front. Pigeonhole introduced me to the driver, Mort (aka "Captain Rehab"), and the rest of the band. Minneapolis seemed like a lifetime away, and as we pulled onto the highway I braced for a drawn-out, robust discussion of the gospel. Or at least temptation, sin, and the promise of redemption. Or whatever Pigeonhole talked about now that he was sober and successful.

"What brings you way out here?" Pigeonhole began.

"Well, Sara broke up with me, and—"

"Congrats, dude! That's huge."

"No, that's bad."

"Oh, sorry. But actually, sometimes ..." He trailed off and appeared to be searching desperately for the right words. Then I realized he was grimacing in pain.

"What is it?" I asked.

"Nothing. It will pass. I mean, this too shall pass."

"Are you still in pain? From the fall? I can't—"

"Don't give it another thought, dude. This is a bus trip, not a guilt trip."

Pigeonhole nodded at his bandmate and mocked scribbling in a notebook. Dutifully he nodded, pulled a pad from his pocket, and took it down. The other band members had found their way to the back of the bus by this point. A few were in bunk beds; one was in a recliner, engrossed in an issue of *Mad* magazine. They had barely seemed to notice my presence. I wondered if Pigeonhole picked up passengers regularly.

"Don't worry about me," Pigeonhole said. "I'm getting great care, making tons of progress. I've got strong movement in both my legs by this point, and they say I'll be able to walk unassisted eventually."

I was thirsty, my mouth dry. He could sense my discomfort.

"Can I get you something? A soda, some water? We're all sober, so no hard stuff."

"Water would be great."

He maneuvered over to a small refrigerator and reached inside. "This is Holy Trinity Spring Water. They're sponsoring the tour, but I would drink it anyway." He handed me the bottle, and I drank down nearly all of it.

"I read your interview in *Rolling Stone*," I said, capping the bottle.

"I didn't know you subscribed." He grinned.

"Impressive, I have to say. Same with your online success. How did all that get started?"

"It started in Tanya's parents' living room, where I was staying after rehab. Tanya has a little sister, and as soon as she saw me shredding on my guitar in my wheelchair, she said, 'This has to be on TikTok!' She was convinced I would become an instant icon. My first video got only six likes, but I thought about those six people all day. Who were they?

Why would they be watching me playing my guitar in a wheelchair in some weird house in Minnetrista, Minnesota, which barely exists on a map, let alone in reality? But those six people were soon sixty and then six hundred and then six thousand and then sixty thousand, and then I was TikTok famous. All thanks to Tanya's little sister. And I didn't even know she had a sister!"

"Kids today," I said.

"I'm making it sound easy, but that's because it was. The hard part is everything else."

"I'd like to know what changed," I said. "I mean, why didn't the fall just make you even more ..."

"Afraid?"

"I wasn't going to say afraid."

"Well, that's what I was, Dudeman. I was afraid. Afraid of failure, afraid of success, afraid of everything in between. Afraid of my own talent, of wasting it, of being a slave to it. Which I was. I still have to be careful about that. Some days I play for eight or ten hours straight."

"I can relate to that," I said. "Sometimes I paint all day. And all night. For days at a time. I barely sleep. Then a week later I can't do anything except sleep."

"There's so much more to life than that kind of obsession, dude. I have to remind myself of that all the time. Still, if I get really down, I have to play my way out of it. And even though I'm one of the more popular guitarists on TikTok at the moment, I'm definitely not the first, and I for sure won't be the last. In other words, humility goes a long way toward keeping the house from becoming haunted."

"Speaking of haunted," I said, "you mentioned in the interview that you had a vision of Jimi Hendrix. Do you think it was really him?"

"I kind of do, yes."

Somehow that wasn't what I wanted to hear. "Have you ever had any other visions like that? Anyone other than Jimi?"

"Let's see. Well, in the old days, I once hallucinated the hell out of a bunch of snakes. But never any people. Or spirits. Or whatever. Why?"

"But you do believe in the spirit world—that some of us are able to see into it?"

"Sure. But I don't have all the answers. No one does."

Something came over me. Maybe it was the cross dangling from Pigeonhole's neck, swinging to the rhythm of the road, half-hypnotizing me into a confession.

"Sometimes ..." I let the thought trail off, but I wasn't certain I could let it go completely.

"Sometimes?"

"It's my mother. Sometimes I see her. Like a ghost. Or a vision."

Pigeonhole sat straight up, supporting his weight with his forearms. "Where?"

"Everywhere."

"How often?"

"Not all the time. But often enough. Too often." I immediately regretted telling him all this.

Pigeonhole went uncharacteristically silent. He closed his eyes and made the sign of the cross in front of his chest. After a minute or so, he opened his eyes again, looking at me as if for the first time.

"If you ask me, visions like that are about forgiveness."

"Forgiveness?"

"The search for it, anyway. We all want to be forgiven. And, as hard as it can be to extend it to others, at heart we all want to forgive. I'm not sure there's anything more important in life than forgiveness."

I had no response to that, and I didn't want to dwell on it. If there was ever a moment I needed to change the subject, it was then.

"So, do you get other free stuff besides spring water?"

Pigeonhole began to name a litany of sponsors and all the products and services he'd received during his meteoric rise to fame: Marshall amplifiers, Ibanez guitars, Shure earphones, Rode microphones, Panasonic video gear, clothing from various companies, jewelry, even food—steaks, soda, barbecue sauce, pickles.

"But it's not about the stuff, or the fame, or the money, or the potential of more money. It's about the music."

I thought of my mother again. "My mom loved music," I said. "Even Van Halen. I think Eddie was a guilty pleasure for her."

"Moms are the fucking best."

"She wasn't really into lead guitar, though. I'm not either, if you can believe it."

"I never would have guessed!" He laughed, then coughed. "Actually, I don't remember ever hearing you listening to music. What's your jam?"

"My jam is usually silence. Sometimes I listen to music, but I don't really listen much. At least not anymore. The music I like reminds me too much of my mother. She played music all day every day, usually while working on her artwork."

"Might be a way for you to share something new with her. Maybe that's why she's still around."

"Maybe." I wasn't so sure.

Pigeonhole sat up in his chair and cleared his throat, as if he were about to take the stand in his own defense.

"But in your case," he began, "I think her presence is more about you than it is about her."

Now he had my undivided attention.

"When you're working, it's just you and your tubes of paint, and a sheet of canvas, and some brushes, and whatever happens to be in your head that day, even if it's your mom's ghost. But no one can do that work for you, not even your mom. No matter how much it seems like she's there trying save you, it's not possible. The real lesson, ultimately, is that only you can save yourself."

I thought about all the times I had seen my mother working on a painting for me, or at least had seen the evidence she had done so. Now Pigeonhole was making me question all of that. I thought for a moment.

"Can you keep this a secret, by the way. I've never told anyone before. It feels weird."

"Your secret is safe with me, dude. Unless I fall off the wagon, that is."

"I hope that doesn't happen."

"For both our sakes."

With that, we moved on to other topics until, after three amazingly quick hours, the bus pulled up in front of my apartment. The street was empty of traffic, and the Time-Warp had just closed. A blue light in my apartment suggested the television had turned itself on.

Mort opened the door, and Pigeonhole rolled toward the lift gate. "The scene of the century right here, dude." He pointed at the door, behind which was the bottom of the staircase where he had landed.

"Again, I'm so sorry," I said in a near-whisper.

Pigeonhole shook his head. "Whether you meant to nor not, you did me a huge favor that day. I hope I did the same for you tonight."

My throat tightened, and for a moment, I couldn't speak.

"Before we call it even, though," Pigeonhole said, "do you happen to know the whereabouts of one cardboard Eddie Van Halen? I was hoping to reunite with the source."

"I don't," I lied. I wasn't sure why I lied. I felt as if I wasn't ready to give him up, but I wasn't sure what that feeling meant. "Tanya might know."

"Oh, jeez. Captain Rehab!" Pigeonhole turned toward Mort. "Turn the bus around! We forgot Tanya in Bayfield!"

I was shocked.

"Just kidding, dude! Tanya's on a spiritual retreat in South Dakota. Don't worry, she's still part of the show. Speaking of which," he said, reaching into his pocket, "take these." He handed me two tickets for a concert at First Avenue in January. "If you make up with Sara, you can bring her. If not, maybe put the second ticket on Craigslist. It's sold out, and they're going for a hundred bucks a pop."

"I can't speak for Sara," I said, "but I'll be there."

"Email me if you find Eddie." He handed me his card. His email address was duderonomy@pigeonhole.god.

I thanked him and stepped off the bus with all my things. I took one last look at Pigeonhole, and he gave me the rock-n-roll sign with both hands. The door closed, the bus pulled away, and the music resumed.

Upstairs, my apartment seemed emptier, lonelier, more haunted than ever. I dropped everything next to my bed and fell asleep as soon as my head hit the pillow.

CHAPTER 31

A FEW WEEKS passed. I half-expected to be paid a visit by Clarissa, or Sara, or even Einstein himself—or possibly the police—but none of that happened. Not even my mother paid me a visit. This was the longest stretch of not seeing her, or any evidence of her, that I'd experienced for years. Just when I thought I might never hear from anyone ever again, I received an email from Dr. Karlsen telling me he was finally ready for me to pick the color for his office. I gave him a call, and we set a time to drive to the paint store together that same afternoon.

He pulled up in front of the TimeWarp, arriving nearly ten minutes early, idling his BMW as I watched him from my apartment window. Who was this guy? I thought. Of all people, why would he be the one to stay in contact? I'll just make a few more strokes on this painting of my mother, I thought. He could wait for that, couldn't he? After all, it wasn't my idea to do this color-picking business.

When I was satisfied, I covered the painting with a sheet and clamped it in place. I hoped my mother would take the hint and let me finish the painting by myself. If I needed her help, I would ask for it by leaving the work exposed. Once I had the clamps in place, I headed downstairs.

"William, you look like you've seen a ghost," Dr. Karlsen said.

This caught me off guard. I didn't have an appropriate answer. "Yes ... I've seen a ghost!" I blurted in a voice that nearly betrayed I meant it.

"You've got a great sense of humor, and for this you'll reap great rewards in due time. But for now, polish your glasses. We'll need every ounce of your optical prowess."

"Don't worry," I said. "The color is going to jump right out at me."

When we arrived at the store, my mother was there and had already chosen the color for me. She pointed at the swatch and then disappeared. This made my choice so easy—and so quick—I worried Dr. Karlsen might not take me seriously. Instead, he simply took the swatch, handed it to the clerk, and ordered two gallons of the color along with a bunch of painting supplies.

When he dropped me off at home, he pulled out his checkbook and wrote a check. As he folded it and pressed it firmly into my hand, he gave me a stern look.

"William, you're a fine young man. Somewhat distracted, I suppose, but not without reason. But above all, you've got resolve. You're resolved to your art. Your passion. Because of this, I promise everything will work out in the end. Think of this check as a down payment on that promise."

I was at a loss for words. Dr. Karlsen must be losing it, I thought, or hiding something. I unfolded the check. It was for $2,000, more than I would have received for one of my best paintings.

"Remember, money isn't everything, eh?" He punched me playfully in the shoulder. "But love—now that's some-thing special. And I'm here to tell you that my daughter will love you until the day you die."

This statement was utterly shocking. I started to speak, but he silenced me with a motion of his right index finger.

"And while I may not be a traditionalist in every sense of the word, I feel it's my duty to honor the role of a father seeking a good mate for his child."

At this point I thought maybe he had lost his mind. "What are you talking about?"

"I'm talking about love! I guess that's pretty dang traditional now that I think about it. But I'm comfortable I've made the right decision." He tapped his head with his index finger. "Or maybe I'm as mad as a hatter! Either way, love isn't something to be taken lightly. Honor her, and she will honor you back." Dr. Karlsen looked up and bellowed an almost frightening laugh. His eyes twinkled, dark and mysterious, like two night skies.

None of this made sense. "Who are you talking about?"

"I'm talking about Sara, of course!"

"You do realize Sara broke up with me months ago, right? And that she basically thinks I'm insane?"

He brushed this aside with a wave of his hand. "Don't worry yourself about all that. It's obvious that Sara, for better or worse, is struggling to figure things out. That could hardly be more clear. But in you, I believe, Sara has found the perfect match."

"You're serious?"

"As a heart attack!" He pounded the steering wheel. "William, you aren't someone who understands things quickly. That's your special charm. You figure things out slowly, over time. Or maybe someone simply informs you, like I just did. But don't worry. There will always be people like you, people searching deeply for understanding and not easily finding it. Least of all in America, I guess, but even here, even now, people have a desire to understand, the way physicians do.

The way artists do. And understanding will come to you in time."

It sounded like a manifesto. "How much time is this going to take exactly?"

"Well, you'll have to wait for Sara to figure her shit out. But believe me. I've been hinting around. Hopefully it won't be forever. In any case, I'm hoping you'll be the first to reach out."

"What about Einstein?"

"I'm sensing you're not entirely convinced. Let me tell you a story. The story of how my wife and I got back together, even after another man, a fucking colleague of mine, impregnated her. Do you want to hear this story?"

"I'm not sure."

"It's relevant, believe me. In fact, Einstein reminds me a bit of that jerk, now that I think about it. All cocksure and presumptuous, like most doctors. But he wasn't even a surgeon! Anyway, you can imagine how much bitterness there was between Shelley and me by then, how much contempt, how much stinging regret. She had moved out, we were suing each other, fighting over the littlest things, trying to psych each other out. And for what?"

I shrugged.

"Exactly! For no reason whatsoever! Except, actually, there was a reason. The reason was that we resented each other for not understanding one thing."

"And ... you're going to tell me the one thing?"

"I'm going to tell you the one thing! We resented each other because we had power over each other. The same exact power. And do you know what that power was?"

"Something ... you're about to tell me?"

"That's right. I'm about to tell you! The power we had was that we refused to surrender fully to each other. We refused to go all in when it mattered most. We had avoided it because we didn't want to give up that last little bit of power. Because once you give it up, you can't get it back. I'm talking about commitment that goes way beyond living together, way beyond marriage, way beyond kids. I'm talking about commitment that's like a one-way trip to another planet. You can't just turn around when things get dicey. You let go, and instead of trying to control the journey, you surrender to the journey itself. Make sense?"

"Kind of. What happened after that?"

"Well, Shelley had gotten herself into a situation that she thought was going to right her ship and sink mine, so to speak. Though she wouldn't have put it into words as such. And yes, with the pregnancy, I felt like I was about to lose her for real. I was essentially forced to let go. I had no other sane choice. Then one day she came to the house unannounced. She said she was there to pick up some things for Sara's bedroom. We ended up in the kitchen, talking. She told me Dr. Asshole didn't want the baby. He had some other shit going on on the side, some nurse or something, but that's beside the point. The point was, she wanted him to be all in, and he wasn't. She told me this matter-of-factly. No crying, hardly any emotion at all, in fact. And then she said something I'll remember until the day I die. Maybe longer."

"And ... you're going to tell me what that thing is?"

"No! I'm not! It's private. But I will tell you this: That was the moment I finally surrendered. Because for fuck's sake, William, if you're not coming together, if you're not spending all your waking, breathing, and sleeping hours coming together with the one you love, over and over and over, then guess what?"

"Just tell me."

"I will tell you! If you're not coming together, over and over and over, then you're falling apart. Farther and farther apart. Little by little. Every single day. And there isn't a damn thing you can do about it."

Not knowing how else to express my bewilderment, I simply nodded.

"Now," he said, turning his body to face me squarely. "I have an actual secret to impart to you. Believe it or not, I once knew your mother."

My jaw went slack, and he started waving his hands briskly.

"Don't worry, William! I'm not your father or anything like that. It was another man who knew her in that way, not me. And I have no idea who that was, I'm afraid. But, I did know her before you were in the picture. She worked at a hospital where I occasionally performed surgeries and where you were born. Oddly, I kept a picture of her all these years. More oddly, at the moment, I can't find the photo. So I can only tell you what I knew of her. Which, other than knowing her professionally, is not much. Except for this. She was particularly interested in the patients with no chance of survival. She spent an inordinate amount of time with them. And, after they had passed on, she was known to linger with the body for ten, twenty, even thirty minutes."

"Why did you never tell me this?"

"I know talking about your mother is a difficult subject for you."

I am going to tell him, I said to myself. Tell him I see her—her ghost, or her image in my head, or something in between. I looked in the back seat to make sure she wasn't there. To my great relief, she wasn't.

"One more thing," he continued. "Your mother once spoke to me of her ability to see spirits of the dead. In the hospital ward, the cafeteria, the parking garage, even the elevators. For some reason, she relayed this information to me on the last day of my contract there." He shifted in his seat.

"William, I need to ask you. Did your mother, when you were young—and forgive me for prying—ever relate such stories to you?"

Of course, she did. That and more. "I thought it was just for fun," I said.

"It's not for fun. Not at all. Did you believe your mother at the time, even a little bit?"

"Not back then."

"What about now?"

I hesitated. "Sometimes." He was holding something back, I could tell. He probably knew I was holding something back as well. "But I have a vivid imagination."

"You certainly do." He rubbed his eyes. "We've all lost someone, William. If we're lucky and live long enough, we all experience unspeakable losses." He looked down at the floor of the car. "Of course I want to see my wife again—in this life or the next. If there is a next."

"It seems to me like one life is enough."

"Maybe I've said too much," he said, shifting in his seat. "I won't speak of this anymore. But please, consider what I said about Sara. That's all I ask."

I nodded, said goodbye, and stepped out of the car.

Chapter 32

THE PORTRAIT OF my mother was giving me so much trouble that I considered abandoning it almost daily. But I still wouldn't let her touch it, even though, undoubtedly, I could have used her help. I kept the canvas covered with an old bedsheet when I wasn't working on it. I didn't even want my mother to see the painting, let alone get close enough to work on it. I wanted the finished product, however it turned out, to be mine and mine alone. If she had the desire to work on a self-portrait, she should have chosen to live.

My plan was to finish the painting, bring it to Caroline, and let her sell it so I never had to see it again. To know it was out there in the world would be good enough for me. I didn't want to live with it. Maybe my mother would take the hint and move on as well, let me be, haunt someone else for a while. Finishing the painting was my attempt at an artistic exorcism.

But that entire week, instead of working on the portrait, I spent most of my time lying in bed thinking about my mother. I lay motionless for hours at time, staring at the portrait in progress, trying to imagine what her life was like in the days before she died. I wanted to understand what led her to that moment, what compelled her to take that irreversible step. I believed that if I truly understood, I could prevent myself from ever taking that step. But the longer I thought, the less I understood. And how could I paint a subject I had failed to understand? I was stuck. Luckily, the act of painting is a way to get unstuck. Just let yourself paint, I told myself. So, finally, I did.

The next week I received another check from Caroline for most of the rest of the money she owed me. She included a note about a prominent collector in New York who had inquired about my work. Maybe Caroline could sell her the portrait of my mother, I thought, hoping it would motivate me to finally finish it; in any case, it was time to replace my car. After a few days of searching, I found a used car fairly easily, the old-fashioned way, in the want ads of a suburban newspaper. It was another used Volvo station wagon, one in considerably better shape than my previous pile of junk. 112,000 miles, dark metallic blue, black leather seats, and the added charm of a few specks of rust here and there. The woman who owned it had purchased it new over twenty-five years before. She said I had been the only person to respond to the ad, which did not appear anywhere online—only in print. She said the car was pre-internet and it didn't belong online. Her husband had recently died. The car reminded her too much of him, so she was selling it. When I told her I was an artist and would be using the car to move my paintings around, she volunteered to lower the price by $1,000. I committed to buying it without even driving it first.

CHAPTER 33

AFTER THE SUCCESS of my show, Caroline had been selling new paintings as fast as I could make them, about one a week. A few collectors bought work sight unseen. Caroline said it was enough for them to "purchase something from his current series," which meant, to me anyway, that I had run out of ideas. But I had enough lingering debt to pay off that I didn't much care. Each new painting brought in around $500 after Caroline's cut. Not a lot by coastal standards, but a far cry from where I'd been just a few months earlier.

Most were new collectors, people who had never done business with Caroline, which she had predicted would happen. Where these people were coming from, I had no idea. As I cranked out new work, my mother was no longer helping me. I had arrived at a point where it seemed I no longer needed her. With her prior help, I had become more patient, more willing to take chances, more willing to fail. Just as she knew when I needed her help, she knew when to back off, to let me work unsupported. It was invigorating and satisfying, but also terrifying and isolating. Although I still hid my portrait of her, I otherwise left my paints and brushes out to let my mother know I was still willing to let her help me. But for all intents and purposes, our collaboration, if it could be called that, had come to an end.

The portrait of Sara that I had started months earlier captured my attention again. I reworked the background, changing it from an empty diner to the backseat of a car. Somehow this better matched the expression I had done my best to interpret. On the seat next to her, I painted a television—an old black-and-white portable TV with static on the screen. At that point, I felt the portrait was done, and I hung it above my bed. That lasted for two days, and then I took it down and put it in the closet.

Eventually I received yet another check from Caroline and decided to use it to fund an actual studio. I also planned to move. I wanted out of the St. Jude—away from the scene of Pigeonhole's fall, away from the cockroaches, away from the memory of Sara breaking up with me. The breakup was the last thing I wanted to remember, and in that apartment, it was always on my mind.

I kept a few of my mother's old paintings in the closet. I rarely looked at them, but in anticipation of moving, I pulled one out and put it on my easel. This was disorienting since her work was so unlike mine. This particular painting, a self-portrait, was mostly dark red, nearly monochromatic. The image was my mother's head and torso in front of a church surrounded by cobblestones that went off in every direction into the distance. Impasto, lots of knife work, but somehow delicate with feathery detail. It was gut-wrenching to imagine her painting this in the basement of our old house. I wondered where this church was, or if it was even real. Her imagination was vivid enough, and her work convincing enough, that she could have made up a story about a fictional church and convinced anyone that she had attended dozens of sermons there, whether or not the church in question existed. Somehow the more far-fetched her stories, the more believable they were.

I took her painting down and turned my attention again to the in-progress portrait of my mother. It needed so much more work, and without her helping me, I doubted I had the skill to complete it. Looking again at my mother's paintings, I could see Caroline was right. People should have the chance to see her work.

The next morning I drove to the storage locker in the same suburb where my childhood home had been and where I'd been storing my mother's artwork for so many years. The weather had been unseasonably cold, but that morning a warm front moved in. It was sunny and well over 50 degrees by midmorning, almost unheard of for late November in Minnesota. I drove the surface streets instead of taking the highway, and I went out of my way to drive past the spot where our house had stood before it burned to the ground. The rebuilt house looked eerily similar to our old house. As I passed by, I didn't stop or even slow down. I was afraid that if I did, I'd look like a nutcase staring at a house I had never lived in, probably with tears in my eyes. I was also afraid that if I lingered too long, my mother would appear, upset with me and out for revenge. It was too late for me to worry about something like that, but the idea of hurting my mother's feelings still gave me pause.

The storage locker facility, Stagecoach Storage, was a few miles farther. I made a couple wrong turns, having not been there for quite some time. But once there I had no trouble remembering the combination to the stall. It was my mother's birthday, 5-26-62. Immediately I pulled out a few of her landscapes. One in particular depicted a long-abandoned stone wall crossing a stretch of gold prairie, a paddock in the distance, two men in the foreground digging, a treasure map between them. I wondered if I could live without this painting no longer in my possession, even if I only looked at it once a year at most. That was when I realized that if I could live without my mother, I could live without at least some of her artwork.

I emailed Caroline and told her I was coming over with twenty paintings.

When I arrived at the gallery, Caroline met me at the curb.

"I was worried you were kidding."

"There's one condition," I said.

"Name it."

"She gets the main gallery, and I get the adjunct."

"Deal. But I want to see more work. We have to choose the show together."

We shook on it. Caroline's interns helped move the paintings from my car into the empty main gallery space. Perimeter was between shows, so my mother's work sat on display, for the first time in a quarter century, on its own in an actual gallery space. The gallery was brighter, cheerier than I remembered. The midday sun was shining through the front windows. I recalled the night of my opening, all the angst I had experienced over the show, and all the help I had received from my mother. Was I now helping her? I wasn't sure. Other than the aura of her artwork, there was no sign of her.

My mother's paintings, at least the ones I chose to bring, were mostly red, and Caroline loved that.

"These reds are incredible. How did she do it?"

"I don't know exactly. Sometimes she mixed cadmium red with vermilion and alizarin crimson, along with a bit of cadmium orange. I'm scared to even try that. Different red pigments interact differently with yellows and blues. Even more so when you start combining them like she did."

"I need you to write something about all this. People will ask."

I wasn't sure how much I wanted to share. "I'll try. But I don't know all her secrets."

She crossed her arms. "No gallerist would want to admit they owe an artist," Caroline said, "but I'm going to admit it right now. I owe you. This show could get me into *ARTnews*. Even *The New York Times*. But I'm curious. What changed your mind about the paintings?"

"I realized I don't need them anymore. Or, at least, I think other people need them more than I do."

Through the window I saw a BMW pull up to the curb. It was Dr. Karlsen. A moment later he appeared in the gallery doorway.

"I see the artist is present," he said.

"What a coincidence," Caroline chirped. "William, this is Dr. Anders Karlsen. He's one of my best collectors."

"We are," Dr. Karlsen said, "previously acquainted."

"Wonderful," Caroline said. "I'll go get your painting." She retreated into the storage room behind the main gallery.

Dr. Karlsen stepped closer. "William, I need to tell you something important. Outside."

He walked out the door, and I followed him to the side-walk.

"It's Clarissa," he said, turning to face me. "She's gotten herself into a bit of a pickle, to put it mildly. I'm telling you this in strict confidence. Cross your heart and hope to die, and all that." I nodded. He took a deep breath and forced it out. "She's going to be a mother."

"A mother?" My first thought was that mothers appear and disappear before your eyes at will, but I knew Dr. Karlsen didn't mean that.

"Maybe. Possibly. I mean, she's pregnant."

I was shocked. I didn't know what to say.

"There's an additional complication," he said. At this point Dr. Karlsen appeared worried that Caroline would become suspicious, so he quickly blurted out, "Stan's the father. Einstein. He's the father. That fucking moron is the father!"

My brain rattled in my skull. I shook my head like a cartoon character. "I can't believe it."

"That," he said, squinting somewhere down the block, "makes two of us."

"If it's any consolation," I offered, "I think Clarissa will make a wonderful mother." I wasn't sure I believed that, but it was the only thing I could think to say.

"Like her mother before her," Dr. Karlsen said, casting a glance up at the sky.

He patted me on the shoulder. "By the way, I heard what happened at the resort. A little deranged, but still. Congratulations on a plan well executed."

"It wasn't exactly a plan," I said. "It just kind of happened."

"Right. Next time if you don't want it to look like a plan, you might think about leaving the slingshot at home."

"There won't be a next time," I said. "I'm getting out of the revenge business."

"Good thinking," Dr. Karlsen said. "I'll take over from here. One more thing. Stan doesn't know about the pregnancy. Not yet. That's up to Clarissa."

"Wow. Does Sara know?"

"She's the one who told me. You should think about texting her, by the way. Or sexting, or whatever it is you kids do."

"I'm almost thirty."

"Whatever. Anyway, email me. You can come over for dinner. I'll invite Clarissa, and you two can talk about all this."

Why on earth he thought that was a good idea was beyond me. He walked us back into the gallery and turned to the paintings leaning against the walls.

"Jesus. Are these yours?" His tone of voice changed completely.

"I wish. They're my mother's."

"No wonder," he said, clearly astonished as he moved from piece to piece. "Definitely no wonder."

"No wonder what?"

"I wish I could go back in time and—" He shook his head and let the idea go.

Caroline came out with a painting wrapped in brown paper. Dr. Karlsen took it, shook Caroline's hand, then shook mine.

"Until next time," he said. He put the painting in the trunk of his BMW and drove off.

"I didn't know you two knew each other," Caroline said. "He never mentioned anything."

"It's a long story."

CHAPTER 34

AFTER A FEW emails back and forth with Dr. Karlsen, I agreed to dinner at his house the following Friday. He assured me that only he and Clarissa would be there. No Sara. No Einstein. No drama. When I arrived at the house, I felt comfortable for once parking in the driveway. Minimal rust meant minimal embarrassment. Clarissa met me at the door, surprisingly dressed for a formal dinner in a black evening gown, pearl necklace, sequined pumps, and, perhaps most surprisingly, a unique silver ring on each finger. I felt self-conscious about my Adidas hoodie and just-passable dark jeans.

"My father was held up at the hospital," she said through the screen door. "He'll be here in a few minutes."

"So, no dinner?"

"There will be dinner, but I'm making it this time." She opened the door and waved me in.

"That's exciting," I said, half-expecting to see Sara lurking upstairs. "What are you making?"

"You know I'm pregnant, right?"

I tried to do a double take. "I do now," I sputtered.

"And you know who the father is?"

"I could take a wild guess."

"Who told you?"

"Well, I haven't talked to Sara in months, so ..."

"I guess I never asked him not to tell you." She led me up the stairs to the living room. A scent entirely different from the roasted pork penetrated the house. It smelled a lot like pizza, but somehow with Thanksgiving overtones and a hint of fermentation. I couldn't imagine what it was.

"How do you feel about all this, especially about Einstein?" I asked. I didn't see any reason not to be point-blank. It was so bizarre.

"How do I feel?" she challenged, as if how I felt about how she felt was the definition of bullshit. "Why don't you just ask me what you really want to know."

"Well, what I want to know is how this could have possibly happened." I cleared my throat. "By which I mean—"

She took a half-step away from me. "You're a truly talented artist."

"Okay, but—"

"And you're a pretty okay person," she said, almost grimacing. "But you can be obnoxiously self-centered. And you come across as bit too sorry for yourself. Make that way too sorry for yourself."

"What does this have to do with—"

"There are types." She twisted out of her shoes and kicked them across the living room. "Different types of people go together."

"Sure, different types of people go together. Where are you going with this?"

"For example, my mother was my father's type. He was her type. And, for better or worse, Sara is your type. And, probably for worse, you are her type. And Stan is not. That's why you should have been trying a little harder. Make that a lot harder. A lot sooner."

Just then Dr. Karlsen burst through the door and stomped up the stairs. He appeared exasperated, but immediately slipped into the role of gracious host.

"William! So glad you could make it!" He gestured toward the kitchen. "Have you seen my new toy? A pizza oven!"

"We're having pizza, in case you didn't already figure that out," Clarissa added.

"Not just any old pizza, though," Dr. Karlsen said. "It's my late wife's lefsa crust sauerkraut potatiskorv pizza. An old family recipe. Not my family. Maybe not even her family. Someone's family."

"It has anchovies and pineapple," Clarissa said. "And the cheese is mostly Jarlsberg." She led us into the kitchen. The new oven was puffing away as she opened the door. "Looks about done." Wielding a giant wooden spatula that resembled a cartoonish canoe paddle, she pulled out the sizzling pizza. The sauerkraut, blackened at the edges, looked like leather shoestrings strewn across a molten bed of bubbling cheese.

"Not a gourmet meal by any stretch," Dr. Karlsen said, "but I think you'll approve. Excuse me a second." Dr. Karlsen moved briskly from the kitchen down the hallway to the bathroom. If I was ever going to get any more information from Clarissa, it was now or never.

"So can you tell me what the hell happened?" I asked.

She closed the oven door while holding the spatula up like a picket sign. "I went up to the resort for a couple days to hang out with Sara and Stan, just for fun. I rented my own cabin—the same one you were in—not long after you were there. You forgot a painting there, by the way. A portrait of a woman talking on the phone."

"Oh, that. It's not really mine. I left it on purpose."

"It's great. Anyway, Sara and Stan were expecting me of course, but they had apparently been fighting for days, and they didn't want to hang out. I planned to just keep to myself. I had wanted some alone time anyway, so I didn't mind. But late on the second night, Stan knocked on my cabin door. He'd been drinking. To be honest, so had I. He said he and Sara were still fighting and he couldn't figure out what was wrong. We started talking, one thing led to another, and …"

That was it? There must have been more to it than just being drunk and stupid, I thought. Had she been after Einstein the entire time? I wasn't going to ask her, but still.

"Is this even remotely what you want?"

"It's a bit more complicated than that, dummy."

"And what about Stan?"

"Well, he's closing the shop permanently and—"

"I mean, what about you and Stan?"

"I haven't told him yet."

"Christ. When are you going to tell him? Are you even going to tell him?"

She fished in a drawer for the pizza cutter. "This is getting a little too personal," she said. As usual, she was right.

Dr. Karlsen returned, now dressed in a polo shirt and jeans. Clarissa proceeded to slice the pizza. We sat down at the dinner table as if it were one of his elaborate meals. The pizza was fantastic, but I didn't say anything. I didn't need to.

"I've never seen you eat like this," Dr. Karlsen said to me. "I'm not going to take it personally. Clarissa is an excellent cook. Like her mother."

Behind Clarissa, the wall where the mirror had been was bare.

"What happened to the mirror?" I asked.

"Sadly," Dr. Karlsen said, "it fell a second time—for what reason, I don't know—and shattered. I had to have a cleaning crew come out and vacuum up all the tiny shards."

"Were you home at the time?"

"Yes. I was here at the table, alone," he said. "There seemed to have been nothing to precipitate the fall. But, thinking back, I did experience a curious sensation just before the mirror fell. Out of nowhere, I had a strong feeling that I should redecorate the house. Spruce it up one last time before I retire." He looked down at his hands. "Which could be anytime. There are so many great young surgeons now. My hands aren't what they used to be. That was my thought just before the mirror fell—that I'm no longer needed."

"This time there wasn't a pork roast on the floor to break the fall," Clarissa said.

Dr. Karlsen stood and went into the kitchen. He returned with three cups of chocolate gelato. We ate in silence. At this point, I still wasn't sure exactly why I had been invited.

Dr. Karlsen pulled his napkin from his lap and set it on the table.

"I know you were a real friend to Pigeonhole," he began.

I expected some expression or gesture that would shed light on the absurdity of what he had just said. But his face was blank, his body motionless. He stared at the wall where the mirror had hung.

"What makes you say that?" I asked.

"He told me himself."

"When did you talk to Pigeonhole?"

"I consulted on his case recently. We were looking at the way he's progressing, considering another surgery, and we got to talking. He told me a few things."

"What did he say?"

"It was a privileged conversation, of course. But I can tell you what you already know. He said you used to let Tanya sleep on your floor when he was too drunk or high for her to be in the same apartment with him. He said you kept her safe."

It was true, though I had never told anyone about that. I wasn't sure if that made me a good friend, though. "I let her use my sleeping bag a few times. That's all."

"He was appreciative, to say the least. He said if not for you, Tanya might have left him."

"That might have been the right thing to do at the time," I said.

"Maybe so," Dr. Karlsen agreed.

"Nice going, William," Clarissa said. "I didn't take you for a humanitarian."

"I mainly did it to separate them, like children, so I could get some sleep. I'll do anything for a few hours of peace and quiet." I probably shouldn't have said that. Why snatch defeat from the jaws of victory? "I wonder where Pigeonhole lives at this point." I, for some reason, assumed Dr. Karlsen would know.

"He said he has a townhouse in Chanhassen, near where Prince used to live. Apparently he goes to Paisley Park once a week to pay his respects."

"I'm sorry I asked," I said. "And that's quite the flip-flop, considering how much he used to hate Prince." The sugar from the gelato was making me dizzy. The dining room seemed off-kilter, and I half-expected the mirror to magically reappear on the wall or maybe materialize in midair right in front of me.

"Seems wrong that it's gone, doesn't it?" Dr. Karlsen said. I'm not sure how he knew I was thinking about the mirror.

"Things come and go," I said. "Just like that. Poof!"

Clarissa laughed. "Poof!" she repeated. "Like Stan's hair."

They both laughed. Dr. Karlsen stood and cleared away the dishes. Clarissa, despite her usual efforts to appear generally pissed off, seemed pleasantly satisfied. I wasn't sure if it was the gelato, the pizza, or something else.

Returning to the dining room, Dr. Karlsen said, "I have an early surgery tomorrow morning, so I'm afraid I have to call it a night." He gestured for me to rise, which I did. I took one last look at the wall where the mirror had hung.

Clarissa remained seated, staring right at me, not changing her expression of satisfaction one iota. I didn't think she could maintain it, even if it was real, particularly if she were putting on airs. There was a moment when I expected her to start giggling, or move to the piano and burst into song, or even break down crying. For Christ's sake, she was carrying Einstein's baby. How could she not be having a nervous breakdown? But instead, barely moving, she whispered something to herself, something I couldn't make out. Then her expression did change, subtly, to something more like acceptance than satisfaction. Her cheeks relaxed, as if someone had told her something she had always wanted to hear. But just as I was about to ask her what she had mumbled, Dr. Karlsen led me down the stairs and outside, and for the first time that evening, I sensed something, or I should say something else, was wrong. Dr. Karlsen closed the door and stood facing me on the stoop.

"I have to tell you something, though I hadn't planned to reveal it to you so soon." Dr. Karlsen appeared to be looking right through me, into the future. "First of all, I'm the collector who purchased all of the artwork from your exhibition."

I realized I had subconsciously intuited this, but I was surprised to hear it directly from him.

"I own over twenty-five of your paintings. I've given a few as gifts, but the bulk of them are being stored in the second guest bedroom upstairs. I look at them often, and they bring me great joy. Having said all that, I hope I didn't interfere with your developing additional collectors."

This was one of the few times I had ever seen Dr. Karlsen appear in any way vulnerable, as if he had committed some type of impropriety. "No, not at all," I said. "In fact, the opposite happened. Caroline asked for more work and has been selling everything I can crank out."

Relief washed over him. "I'm so glad to hear that," he said. "I see you have a new car as well. Well, new to you, anyway. I once had a similar Volvo. That thing would still be kicking if I hadn't crashed it the week after my wife passed away. I shouldn't have been driving. Anyway, good on you. It's a nice car."

"Volvos last forever," I said. This was something I knew to be untrue, having had one die on me recently, but it sounded so suburban that, given the context, I felt compelled to say it.

"So true. I wish I could say the same about fucking BMWs." Dr Karlsen shifted his feet and looked up the block toward the BP. "I have something else to confide in you. Please, keep this to yourself for now."

The wind picked up. It had begun to snow lightly, and my car windshield was covered in a dusty layer of flakes. Dr. Karlsen reached out to grasp my forearm.

"William, I'm dying."

"What do you mean, dying?"

"I have cancer. It's terminal. Treatment or not, it's so far progressed I have maybe six months."

Flakes of snow landed on my glasses. There were tears in Dr. Karlsen's eyes.

"I'm so sorry," I said. "Do Sara and Clarissa know?"

"Not yet." He let go of my arm. "I'm leaving my practice at the end of the month and will tell them as soon as I can get them both together. Maybe tomorrow or the day after. I have to do it in person, with them both here at home. There's no other way."

"So you're telling me first?"

"Imagine telling your daughters that you're dying."

I could not imagine that. "Is there anything I can do to help?"

"While I don't expect you to suddenly propose to Sara or anything like that, as I said, my hope is that you'll get together eventually. When you're both ready."

"When will we be 'ready'?" I made air quotes, which I immediately realized was rude under the circumstances.

"Maybe when you realize that you were never really in love with Sara to begin with? That you only thought you were? That you confused love with obsession? That maybe this is your chance to figure it all out?"

That diatribe made me cringe. It was like hearing something directly from Carl Jung, something that was inarguable, but not something you would conceive of on your own. Still, I couldn't really say he was wrong, so I said nothing.

"I may be pressuring you," he said, "but not into something you don't want. I would at least like to know that you'll consider reaching out to her. Maybe not right away. But soon."

I could see the pain in his eyes and hear it in his quivering voice. I couldn't say no.

"Of course," I said. "Of course I will."

"Thank you."

"I'm not entirely convinced she wants to hear from me though. I mean, she left me for Einstein."

"He's taken care of that little problem for you now, hasn't he?"

"I guess he has," I said. "But that's not the whole story."

"Nothing's ever the whole story."

"What I mean is, I have something I want to tell you, too." I said this without really knowing what I was about to say.

I had Dr. Karlsen's full attention. It was too late now.

"Sometimes, I ... I mean, often ..." I trailed off.

Dr. Karlsen wiped his eyes.

"I have visions."

"Visions? Well, you are an artist."

"Not those kinds of visions." The service station sign glowed brightly at the end of the block, reflecting off my glasses. "I mean, I see my mother. It's like her ghost or something. At least, that's what I think it is. Or maybe I'm just imagining things. Maybe I'm more like her than I want to admit."

"For how long?"

"Years. More than half my life at this point."

Dr. Karlsen's face went blank for a moment, and then tears came again. "These kinds of visions are not so unusual," he said. "In some cultures, it's considered a gift to see people on the other side of death. To be fair, I think in most cultures it's considered a gift. Sometimes even in this one." He gestured around. "What's less common is people admitting it."

"So you don't think I'm crazy?"

"I'm a surgeon, not a psychiatrist. But in my professional opinion, I'd say you're a lot like most people. You see what you need to see. I would never call that crazy."

I appreciated that, but I didn't know how to respond.

"I'll invite you back soon," he said, "but for now I think it's best for my daughters and I to spend some time alone. There will be a lot for us to talk about. Decisions to be made and so on. You do understand?"

I nodded. After a moment of silence, he held out his hand, and I shook it. He reentered his house, leaving me on the steps, staring down at my boots just as I had done on the night of the explosion. Time for a new pair of boots, I thought. Back in my car, I sat thinking about the information Clarissa and Sara should have received before I did. There was nothing I could do to help them. All I could do was prepare. Prepare to be available. Prepare to listen. They had already lost their mother, but this would be different. This would be final. I was familiar with final.

I started the car, and the headlights popped on, illuminating the block. Other than the service station fire, not much had changed on that street in the past year or so since I'd been visiting. But change was coming.

As I drove past the new BP, the memory of seeing my mother there—by way of the television—compelled me to stop. I pulled up to the pumps to get gas and look around the rebuilt station. While the tank was filling, I tried to envision my mother walking through that giant fireball, holding court in her way, as only she could. As I hung up the pump and replaced the gas cap, I asked myself: Was Dr. Karlsen right? Had I never been in love with Sara in the first place? That was a hell of a thing to say. But maybe, as he had suggested, it was time for me to find out what love really meant.

CHAPTER 35

Dr. Karlsen's admonition for me to contact Sara resurfaced memories I had spent a great deal of effort trying to repress. Not that I, a born ruminator, was ever all that successful at repressing my thoughts about Sara. As an example, there was the time—a bit before things started turning sour between us—that she informed me of a phone call she had received the day before.

"My old boyfriend called me last night," she said with the delivery of a stand-up comedian.

"Which old boyfriend?"

"Stan. The one I told you about. He said he found a pair of my underwear beneath his bed and asked if I wanted them back."

At the time, I had only heard of Stan in passing. I could not for the life of me figure out why she would be telling me this. It didn't make any sense at the time, but now I think maybe she was hoping a spark of jealousy might light a fire inside me.

"What did you tell him?"

"I told him to send me a picture."

"Did he?"

"He sure did."

"And then?"

"They weren't mine."

One of Sara's superpowers had always been to never, ever laugh at anything funny she said. Another of her superpowers was her absolute unwillingness to open a social media account of any kind. I was in awe of this power, because I had, in my mind, no choice but to post my artwork to Instagram, even if half my posts ended up with only a handful of likes. Or none at all. And I spent an inordinate amount of time trying to get the lighting ideal, the colors accurate, and the details sharp. It was a waste of time in hindsight, but at least I was trying. It was preternaturally wise of her to actively avoid the greatest time suck the world has ever seen. She would occasionally lord this over me, especially when I used my need for more studio time as an excuse for us not to hang out. "Paint more, post less," she said to me on more than a few occasions.

As far as I could tell, Sara's relationship with Clarissa had always been somewhat fraught, but even now—even after Einstein's utter betrayal—I could imagine Sara putting this turn of events into perspective. She might even embrace it, depending on how things turned out. Maybe she'd become an aunt. Maybe everyone would live happily ever after. Who could say? Regardless, Sara would handle it her way. Of this there would be no doubt. Where there was some doubt, though, was in how she might handle hearing from me again.

Which brings me to some of her less admirable traits. She liked to wake me up in the middle of the night to ask me questions. Not deep or important questions, like whether I really loved her, or maybe whether I meant all the things I said about her when we were making love. Instead it was things like, "Wake up. I think I left my purse on the seat of your car. Can you go out and check? No, wait, here it is." I guess that's not so bad. But at the time I couldn't understand where she was coming from. My thought was, why rely on me? That will never work out, and we both know it.

A less admirable trait turned out to be that she often texted with Stan, pretty much the entire time we were dating. At least she was open about it. I tried to look the other way, but there was always something about it that I hated. It didn't matter, I told myself. But suddenly one day it was all that mattered.

Aside from all the memories of her, I thought back on all the selfish and inconsiderate things I had done, especially toward the end. Most of it was the result of putting my artwork first and my relationship with her third or fourth. Also vying for first place was, by definition, my relationship with my dead mother, which, to be fair to myself, was a priority but not by choice. This haunting was the cause of much of my selfish and inconsiderate behavior. I was in no position to think clearly, act rationally, or emote intelligently. After all of that, it wasn't surprising Sara had had enough of me. I had had enough of me, too, and in fact Sara had been the charitable one.

If I was really going to reach out to her, as her father was berating me to do, would I be returning as the charity case I always had been? Or would all that had occurred with Einstein in the interim be enough to at least open the door to new possibilities?

CHAPTER 36

AFTER A FEW glimmers of hope, progress on the portrait of my mother had again stalled. Up to that point, she had respected my wishes and not interfered with the work. In fact, she had gone completely missing—it had been weeks since I'd seen her. I was on my own. Sadly, it showed. The portrait was far from my best work, and I didn't know how to go about improving it. The painting needed a new direction, a change that I couldn't conceive of on my own, let alone execute.

At one point, I had painted a tube of lipstick in her hand, then removed it, then put it back, then replaced it with a popsicle—one of the red, white, and blue "rocket" popsicles she kept on hand when I was a kid. I think she liked them more than I did. Still, the popsicle looked ridiculous, so I got rid of it. I replaced it with the tone arm from a record player, loose wires dangling from one end. A scratch on her cheek indicated she had turned the needle on herself. I wasn't sure if any of this would remain in the final portrait, but at least I was exploring ideas. Late one night, I considered leaving the portrait uncovered to see if my mother would take the hint and either approve of, or remove, the recent changes. But I decided against it. I wanted to be absolutely sure I had exhausted all my creativity.

A week had passed since Dr. Karlsen told me he was dying. I imagined he had told his daughters by now. Before I was able to work up the nerve to call Sara, she sent me a text message asking, rather formally, if I could meet her at the TimeWarp later that night. She said she had some news. I texted her back, saying I was working on a painting, but could be there around seven. The truth was, I didn't work on the painting at all. I just sat there for hours worrying that I would say or do something unbearably stupid as soon as I saw Sara in person again, like tell her I was never in love with her—whether or not that was even true, though I was certain it wasn't.

Just after seven that night, I entered the TimeWarp. Sara was sitting at the rear of the bar at our usual table. She wore a dark gray sweater and a black scarf, which, in the bar's low light, bled into the wall behind her, making her head look disembodied. She wore dark red lipstick, heavy black eyeliner, and cerulean blue eye shadow. She had a beer waiting for me at the table, so I skipped the bar and sat down. For a while we just sat in silence. I closed my eyes and began to hum along with Nick Lowe's "Cruel to Be Kind" coming from the jukebox.

"Did you pick out this song?" she asked. "Sounds like your kind of thing."

I shook my head. "I just got here. Must have been someone else."

From his barstool, the building's caretaker, Enrique, waved at us. At the pool table, someone racked and broke, and a game began. I searched the barroom for my mother, but she was nowhere to be seen. I saw only the usual patrons, the bartender, and my own reflection in a Grain Belt–

emblazoned mirror. I had Pigeonhole's concert tickets in my pocket. I pulled them out and set them on the table.

Sara picked one up and held it to the light of her phone. "Seriously?"

"First Avenue. One night only."

"Where did you get these?"

"He gave them to me himself."

"He's back?"

"He's not back back. There's no elevator in the building, for one thing. Plus, he's making money now. He has no reason to live here. But they haven't rented the apartment to anyone else yet, which is great for me."

"I'm sure you're getting a lot done," Sara said with some degree of charity.

"Hopefully another insane musician won't move in." I took a sip of the beer and held my ticket next to hers, as if to compare two similar scientific specimens. "So, are you in?"

She put her ticket in her purse. "I'll think about it."

I put my ticket in my back pocket and shifted in my seat. "You said you had some news?"

She took a deep breath. "It's bad," she said. "It's about my father."

The bar was cold, and I shivered as I waited for her to go on.

She put her hands to her face. "He has cancer. Liver cancer. And it's spreading. He says they might be able to slow it down, extend his life a few months, but it's terminal."

She didn't know he had told me, that much was clear. The proper thing for me to do would have been to say I was sorry, and of course I was. But I wasn't sure whether to pretend to be surprised or admit he had told me first. I should have run through this in my head beforehand. Instead, I just stared at her. Then a strange thought occurred to me. What if my mother had told me she was "dying" before she had done what she did? Would it have helped? I realized then that it might have.

"I'm so sorry. Does Clarissa know?"

She seemed to be waiting for me to explain my lack of surprise, but I didn't want to add to the injury.

"He told us both at once," she said, "the night before last."

Sara swirled her glass of beer, then let it settle. "My father told me something else. Something—"

Sara abruptly stopped speaking and shifted her gaze toward the front of the bar. Judging by the look on her face, I imagined she was seeing my mother for the first time.

Instead, when I turned around, I saw Einstein at the door wearing an orange jumpsuit and holding a bright orange pistol. I immediately realized it was a flare gun, but I wondered if he knew that. In the low light, he didn't see us right away. He just stood there like some kind of deranged plastic Ken doll. I knew he was there for me, and I considered jumping up and running out the back door, but that would have been too cowardly, even for me. Instead, I bolted upright and faced him. He spotted me and charged our table.

"Don't move, asshole!" he snarled, pointing the gun at me.

Sara shot up and sidestepped toward the bar in a panic. I held my hands above my head in a gesture of mock surrender. With a quick nod, I urged Sara to run. She did, out the back entrance.

Einstein fixed his gaze on me and appeared not to see Sara at all.

"Motherfucker, this is for shooting me in the balls!"

He trained the gun at my groin and pulled the trigger. Nothing happened. He tried again. There was a dull click. Frustrated, he stupidly pointed the gun at his face and looked down the barrel, then aimed it at the ceiling. When he pulled the trigger a third time, the gun discharged. The flare punctured the old tin ceiling, and sparks shot from the hole like blood spurting from a wound. Again Einstein pointed the gun at me and fired, but it was a single shot flare. He threw the gun down, and I lunged at him as fast as I could, going straight for his hairpiece. He bear-hugged me and bit me on the ear. It hurt so much I worried that he had torn off my ear and that it would end up in a jar behind the bar. We grappled and fell to the floor, landing next to Enrique's boots. Enrique drew his boot back and prepared to deliver a blow to Einstein's head.

"This isn't about you!" Einstein yelled at Enrique. Enrique apparently agreed and held back. Einstein kneed me in the chest, squirmed out of my grasp, and ran for the door.

Enrique picked up the flare gun. "I've always wanted one of these," he said. He stuffed the gun into his pants and took off out the front door. I staggered to my feet and ran behind him as a fire alarm sounded. Out on the sidewalk, Enrique had pinned Einstein to the ground. Einstein appeared to be in tears.

Soon there was smoke coming from my apartment window, which I had left open a crack. Light from the flames lit my apartment. A charcoal hand rapped at the glass from inside—my mother's hand. Sirens sounded in the distance. I hurried over to the building's front door and pulled out my key.

"Stop!" yelled Sara, running toward me from the side of the building. "You can't go up there!" She grabbed my arm. "What the fuck are you thinking?"

I twisted free, got the door open, and wedged myself through. I tried to pull the door closed, but she blocked me.

"William, don't do this!"

"I can't let my entire life go up in flames! Not again!"

"Are you crazy?"

Ignoring this, I ran up the stairs. As I reached the landing, I asked myself if I was making my last mistake. Running into a fire? Potentially trapping myself? But I felt like I had no choice, no more choice than my mother had that day. I had to save my paintings, and my mother's paintings, and maybe my mother herself. Sara looked up the stairwell at me as if for the last time.

There was no going back now. I turned the corner at the top of the stairs and ran past Pigeonhole's door to my apartment. The sound of flames crackled into the hallway, and the smell of turpentine was in the air. The door to my apartment was warm, but not hot. I unlocked it and kicked it open. My worktable and the floor underneath it were on fire. I didn't see my mother anywhere. But worse, the portrait wasn't there. Where could it have gone? The window was now fully open. Instinctively, I dodged past the fire and began to toss everything I could get my hands on out the open window. All my work in progress. Some clothes. The cardboard Eddie. My portrait of Sara. By this point, the flames had spread up the wall, and I knew I was taking a ridiculous chance. An open can of turpentine fell from my worktable and burst into flames, blocking me from the door. The window ledge was the only way out now.

As I desperately hunted for anything else I could save, my mother appeared right in front of me, standing just a foot away. I reached up and wiped a tear from her cheek. Ash from her skin collected on my fingers, reminding me of the Halloween makeup from so many years before. We were now nearly surrounded by flames, but strangely I felt none of the heat, none of the danger I was in.

"If you're really here," I said, "say something."

She moved her mouth, pulling at her hair in frustration, but no words came. She turned around and stepped into the fire, picking up the can of turpentine. She took a whiff from the can. Did she know what she was doing? Did she ever? As if just then realizing what she held, she emptied the can, and the liquid exploded into flames. Her long hair rose, whipping upward, mimicking the fire around her. She shook her head, and ashes fell as she stepped back out of the flames.

"Tell me why you did it," I said. "You need to tell my why."

A few words would have been enough. Even the wrong words. But, like so many times before, she was unable to speak. Instead, she threw her hands up and let out a scream. This seemed to release her from the spell that had kept her silent for so many years. She drew in a breath, and miraculously, in a voice as raspy and dry as kindling, she said, "I loved you more than I could bear." My mother's eyes were the same blue-gray I remembered from when I was a child. Our basement, the record collection, the crazy late nights no school-age child should have been awake to experience, all of it came rushing back.

At long last I could sense her regret, her desire to have made another choice. She turned her head from side to side, as if scanning the room for another ghost, one only she could see. I thought about how it might feel to die the way she had. I turned and leaned out the open window. My mother moved toward me, and we embraced. Together, we stepped through the open window and onto the ledge. She put her hands to her face. Her fingertips were bright red. Not just the nails, but the entire ends of her fingers, as if she had dipped them in red paint. She raked her hands along her face, leaving streaks of crimson across her forehead, nose, and cheeks. She reached out to embrace me again. I held her tight and shut my eyes like coffin lids. I felt for the corner of the ledge with my foot, squeezing my mother so tightly it felt as if her bones were about to snap. We plunged forward from the second story to the sidewalk below.

The fall went on and on and would still being going on if I had my way. It felt like falling from one world into another. But nothing was going to change the fact that we were about to crash into the sidewalk right in front of the door where Pigeonhole had landed and nearly died. My mother hit the ground first. I landed on top of her, the impact knocking me back into the world.

Somehow, I wasn't hurt. And I wasn't on top of my mother. I was on top of her portrait, the painting of her that I had yet to finish. I heard a woman screaming. I realized it was Sara. I managed to stand, and Sara collapsed into me, sobbing. A moment later, she pushed away and ran off around the corner of the building. I didn't follow.

The air was copper, particles of dust and ash reflecting the lights of the emergency vehicles. Steam shot from the windows in thick tufts. The firefighters, amazed I wasn't hurt, turned their attention to dousing my apartment through the window I had just leapt from. In less time than I would have thought possible, they put out the fire before it spread to Vernon's apartment above.

Behind me, Enrique and Einstein were arguing in front of two police officers.

"You know this clown?" one officer asked me.

I nodded.

"We're going to need your contact information."

I gave one of the officers my number as they handcuffed Einstein and put him in the back of a squad car.

"Looks like you managed to nearly destroy my home and, along with it, much of my life's work," Vernon said from behind me, his already low voice an octave lower than usual.

Although I hadn't been the one to pull the trigger, it seemed like the wrong time to take a defensive posture. I hadn't seen him since that night in Wisconsin.

"I'm so sorry this happened," I said. Then, I couldn't help myself: "But it wasn't me. It was Einstein."

"We can't blame everything on poor Albert now, can we?"

"No, the other Einstein."

"I can see him in the squad car, genius. And I was in the bar at the time. You must have really pissed him off."

"I guess so."

Vernon was actually taking it pretty well. "I hope you have renter's insurance," he said bluntly.

That was something I hadn't gotten around to acquiring.

"Either way, I'm glad you're okay," he said, his face a mix of strain and concern.

"Have you seen Sara?" I asked.

"She ran off that way." He pointed across the street.

I looked north toward the 10th Avenue bridge and recalled the time Vernon had offered me a blintz. Then I remembered his UFO sojourn.

"Say, Vernon," I blurted, "did you end up seeing anything that night in Wisconsin, I mean, once you got to the coordinates?"

He dropped his arm as if he were dropping a microphone. Then he took himself and his ever-present suitcase and walked off.

By this time, Enrique was busy dodging firefighters, grabbing all my stuff from the sidewalk and moving it to the curb. He leaned the cardboard Eddie against the bus shelter. "I saw Van Halen in Mexico City in '96," he said, holding his fist to his heart. "It was epic. Now, go get your car. I'll help you load all this shit."

"Enrique, you don't have to do this."

"Willie, you're a good kid. Stubborn, like a grass stain, but a good kid. Now shut the hell up and go get your car."

CHAPTER 37

I WAS AMAZED that everything I now owned—mostly clothes, art supplies, several nearly finished paintings, and one cardboard cutout—fit entirely inside a single vehicle. I drove away, in no particular direction, first wandering downtown, then back up West River Road. It took a few miles of driving to get up the nerve to call Sara. When I pulled over and dialed, she didn't pick up. I tried again. Same thing. I had nowhere else to go, so I started toward her apartment building. On my way across the river, I was filled with dread, as if I were driving across the border of a nation no one had ever returned from—some kind of inner nation, one where you immediately lose all your rights, followed by your property, then your dignity, your identity, your objectivity, and finally your mind.

As I got out of my car, the air was perfectly still. Wishing I had my old key, I rang Sara's apartment. No answer. I thought about ringing Clarissa's apartment but hesitated. I rang Sara's again, and this time she buzzed me in. As I made my way up the stairs, I became overwhelmed with emotion, dizzy, unable to think. At the landing, I bent over at the waist trying to keep from falling faint. I thought about my mother, my portrait of her, how it helped break my fall. I sat down on the stairs, sweating and out of breath.

Sara appeared at the top of the landing. She looked more exhausted than I had ever seen her. Guilt washed over me. I wanted to blame Einstein, but—although he had played a hand in all this—he hadn't forced me into a burning building. With a resigned tilt of her head, Sara gestured for me to come up the stairs and into her apartment. I had not been inside Sara's apartment since the encounter with Einstein months earlier. I was worried he'd come storming out of the bedroom again, still wearing the robe, a banjo strapped over his shoulder, intent on some kind of country-bluegrass-and-blues-infused vengeance. But there was no reason to worry about that. He would quite likely be spending the night in jail.

I sat on the couch. Sara stood at the kitchen counter, saying nothing at first. I wasn't sure if she didn't know what to say or if she was waiting for me to start apologizing.

"Sara, I—"

"Are you fucking insane?" Her voice was quivering. "I can't believe you ran into a burning building."

"I'm not sure 'fucking insane' quite covers it, but at least I survived."

"I'm sorry I ran away. Is the fire out?"

"Yeah, they were able to put it out pretty quickly. I don't know for sure, but other than my apartment, there's probably more water damage than anything."

"I'm glad you got out safe. You and your paintings. I knew you'd throw them out the window eventually. And that you'd jump out after them." Sara turned on the faucet and began to fill a teakettle.

"Cold comfort maybe," I said, "but you called it."

"I also can't believe Stan did what he did," she said. "A flare gun?"

"At least it wasn't a real gun," I said. "He's in enough trouble already."

"Nah. Stan's father is a high-powered attorney with every connection possible. They'll be in court for ten minutes, and he'll end up with community service at worst." She set the teakettle on the stove and turned on the burner.

"Hopefully that court appearance won't involve any testimony from me," I said. "Because there's no way I'm going under oath with Einstein's lawyer in the room. I assume you heard about our little encounter on the lake?"

She dug around in her dishwasher. "You've got the Fifth Amendment on your side, I guess. But not much else. In any case, your feud with him needs to end."

I nodded in embarrassment and relief. "You were about to tell me something when Einstein showed up," I said.

"I wasn't supposed to say anything." She looked over at her reflection in the small mirror on her kitchen wall. "But I'm going to tell you anyway. It's something my father told me."

"Sounds ominous."

"It is, kind of."

"Well, don't keep me in suspense."

"I'm not actually sure you want to hear this."

"Just tell me already."

"Okay, fine. He told me that, recently, when he was home alone staring at the mirror in the dining room, he saw my mother's ghost."

I was stunned. "Really? Did he see anyone else?"

"What do you mean, 'anyone else'?"

"I mean, he just saw her? No other ... ghosts?"

"No other ghosts that I know of."

"When did this happen?"

"When the mirror fell again and broke."

"Why didn't he say anything about it when I was there?"

"A reconstructive surgeon doesn't generally go on about seeing spirits around the house. Plus, my dad's never had anything like that happen before."

"If he told you not to say anything, why are you telling me?"

"Because he said it was something he had in common."

"In common? With who?"

"With you."

That he had betrayed me was something I began to forgive him for immediately, but it was still a blow.

"Is it true?" Sara asked, her voice a whisper. "Do you see your mother's ghost? Or some kind of hallucination? Based on what you did tonight, and all your other weird shit, it definitely seems like it."

I stood up. "I need to take a shower," I said. "I stink, and I'm covered in soot. And I need somewhere to stay. Can I stay here? I don't have anywhere else to go."

Her expression, a mix of shock and fury and regret, practically knocked me over. I wasn't sure if she was going to kick me out, call the cops, or ask me to pay rent. The energy she'd been holding in—for who knows how long—was about to boil over. She turned off the burner under the teakettle, bookmarking this conversation for later. "The bathroom's all yours."

Once I had showered, Sara offered me a pillow and blanket for the couch. She poured two cups of tea and handed one to me.

"I'm thinking about applying to law school, for real this time," she said. She sat on the couch next to me. "It was something my dad always wanted."

"Wanted?"

"Wants. Wanted. Whatever."

"At least your father knows what he wants for you," I said. "I'll give him that." I took a sip of tea. "But what do you want?"

"I don't know what I want. I'm not like my father. And I'm not like you. You always seem to know what you want, even if it's just to be left alone."

I was surprised to hear myself characterized like that, but she was right. "Knowing what you want isn't that great," I said. "Because usually it doesn't work out all that well, at least not in my case."

"My dad said I should apply to a bunch of schools even if I end up deferring or not going. He said something about not knowing what you want until it's gone, and then the opportunity might never come again. That's when he told me about seeing our mother's ghost."

"Do you believe in ghosts?"

"I'm not sure. I mean, I believe that he saw what he thinks he saw. But I'm not sure I believe in ghosts, or spirits, or whatever."

"Have you ever experienced anything like it?" I felt compelled to ask, as if the three of us would now have this curse in common.

Sara thought for a moment. "Once, when I was about thirteen, I turned on the radio, and I thought I heard our mother's voice in the static between stations. It lasted for a few seconds. It only happened that one time. And I've never heard anything like it again."

I could tell by the effort it took her to relay the story that she was telling the truth.

"Did you ever tell your father about that?" I asked.

"No."

"Well, I think you should."

She took a sip of tea. "How has your work been coming along?"

Changing the subject had always been one of her strong suits. I thought for a moment about where to begin.

"Caroline says a New York collector called her. Someone she knew by reputation only. She ended up buying a painting over the phone. Caroline wants me to go meet her. Have lunch with her in New York."

"That's fantastic."

"I've never even been to New York."

"What? How did this never come up before?"

"Never visiting New York isn't really something a person brings up in conversation."

"Well, at least now you have an excuse to go."

"I'm not sure I even want to."

"Why not?"

"I'm not sure why not."

"I can tell you why not." Sara's tone of voice became didactic. "It's because you're the most distracted person on earth. Distracted by your own bullshit. You could paint a house on fire while your house was actually on fire and barely even notice. That's your truth. Going to New York for a week and not being able to paint the entire time would force you to let all that go."

She was right. Again. "Maybe I could use the break," I said. "Or at least some new subject matter other than burned-out houses. I was thinking about maybe switching to UFOs. Could be interesting subject matter. And usually UFOs aren't on fire."

"Spaceships can take a lot of heat," she said. She drew in a deep breath. We sat next to each other on the couch, facing straight ahead, looking at the closed window blinds as if they were a stunning vista.

"That's how your mother died, isn't it?" she asked. "In a fire?"

Of course she figured it out. It wasn't that hard. But for some reason, I never expected her to actually say it. In my mind it shattered some kind of imaginary barrier between us. I didn't dare turn to face her, or I knew that I might lean toward her, let my hand fall onto her shoulder, let my fingers run through her hair.

"I never told anyone that," I said.

"You never said what happened exactly, but—" Her voice was quivering again. "How come you never told me?"

"The fact that my mother set herself on fire isn't something I was eager to share with anyone."

"I'm not just anyone."

"I didn't mean it like that. I meant, once you reveal something like that, you can never take it back."

"Why would you want to take it back?"

"I want to take everything back. I want to go back to before all this ever happened." I started to choke up. "But I can't go back. All I can do is move forward. That means keeping certain things to myself. That's the best I can do."

Sara leaned forward and hit her knee against the coffee table. Her teacup toppled over and splashed on her leg. She went to the kitchen for a towel. I thought I heard my mother chuckle. Startled, I followed Sara into the kitchen. As I approached her, I detected something new in her face, an expression I'd never seen or imagined she could make. Galvanic, determined. Could she have heard my mother's laugh, too? Heard the scrape of a slipper, smelled smoke, tasted ash? For a moment, it seemed possible. The room was warm, and I began to perspire along my hairline. It wasn't much, just enough to make Sara reach up and touch my brow. This broke the spell, and she spoke.

"I'm sorry." This was all she said. "I'm so sorry."

My lips were trembling. "Don't be," I managed to say.

"I am sorry, whether you think I should be or not."

"Okay, then we can both be sorry."

"What are you sorry for?" she asked.

"I'm sorry for being an idiot. And I'm sorry that my being an idiot hurt you. And I'm sorry I didn't do anything about it before now." I had owed her this apology for some time, and after saying it out loud, I understood that it wasn't all I owed her.

"I never thought I'd hear you say anything like that," she declared with the finality of someone sweeping up broken glass. "Thank you."

There is no accurate description of what Sara did next. The best I can say is that she pressed herself against me to, in some sense, read me. She didn't touch me with her hands or arms, but turned her head to the side and placed her cheek on my shoulder. For thirty seconds she let her body read mine. Then, as if she had found a new piece of previously hidden information, she moved her arms up and around my back, her hands behind my shoulder blades, closed her eyes, and kissed me. Only then did I realize just how much I had wanted that to happen.

Chapter 38

THE NEXT MORNING Sara woke up laughing, as if she were coming out of a dream so amusing that she had entirely forgotten the events of the night before. I wished I felt the same way. I wasn't about to remind her. She wrapped herself up in the covers and kept giggling.

"I don't find this situation funny," I said. I had already been awake for nearly an hour, mostly looking at my phone, occasionally gazing at Sara.

"Not yet, you don't." She went silent for a moment and then sat up. "I need to show you something. I'll be right back." She slipped out of bed and shuffled down the hallway.

I thought about my mother. The embrace, the fall, her portrait. None of it seemed real. I felt dizzy for a moment, the bed like an ocean moving beneath me, bizarre creatures swimming deep below the surface, one of which at any time might breach and swallow me up. There were too many unanswered questions. Where was I going to live? Would I ever see my mother again? Would Clarissa have Einstein's baby? How long would Dr. Karlsen live? Long enough to meet his grandson?

I rolled out of bed and opened the window shade. Sara's bedroom faced south, and the morning light was strong, the sky calm. It looked like it would be a quiet day. Across the river I could just make out the roofline of the St. Jude. Though I knew I'd possibly never enter the building again, I was, to say the least, grateful the fire hadn't spread.

I looked around Sara's bedroom. I had never really thought about how small the room was—barely big enough for a double bed, a miniature desk with a tiny laptop, and a tall antique dresser. I couldn't deal with a room this small. It wasn't the lack of space exactly, but the lack of distance from the walls. I needed to get far enough away from my paintings to gain some perspective on them. Or was I just trying to get away from myself? I looked down at the street. My first instinct, always, was to search for my mother, but the street was completely empty.

Sara returned in my old robe, the Pendleton.

"Jesus fucking Christ," I said. "That thing will never die."

"Pendletons live forever." She started undoing the robe. "You want to try it on?"

"Not quite yet," I said.

She redid the robe and sat down on the bed. "Can you imagine me as a mother?" she asked.

"You?" My voice cracked a bit. "Sure, I think you've probably got what it takes."

"Probably?"

"The 'probably' isn't you," I said. "It's me trying to figure out what would make a good mother. I'm like the world's worst expert on that particular topic."

"I'm not so sure," she said. "How about Clarissa? Can you imagine her as a mother? I kind of can't."

"Maybe. But my thought was more about Einstein being a father." I searched around for my socks. "What are they going to do, anyway?"

"They?"

"Yeah, the two of them."

"Stan still doesn't know. I think after what happened last night, he might never know." Sara casually pointed under the bed where my socks were balled up. "It's up to Clarissa in any case."

"Have you two talked?" I asked. "You and Stan, I mean?"

"Not in so many words."

I leaned down and picked up my socks. I imagined paying Einstein another visit to deliver the news myself. Hold onto your hairpiece, you're gonna be a dad! But, recalling that orange gun pointed at me, I was sure I never wanted to see Einstein again.

"Do you think you will?" I asked. "Talk to him, I mean."

"Eventually. But I'm not sure he'll give a shit what I think either way."

"What about you and Clarissa?"

"What about us?"

"I mean, this situation probably isn't something you saw coming."

"My dad says he saw it coming."

"Really?" I was shocked at first, but then I remembered how perceptive he was. "Did he say anything else?" I asked, seemingly from left field.

"Anything else? Like what?"

"Like anything about the two of us?"

She stood up. "Can we get out of here? Go have breakfast, maybe?"

"Good idea," I said. "I'm starving."

While Sara showered, I went down to my car to get the portrait I had painted of her. It was much smaller than the portrait of my mother, just her face on a 2-foot-by-2-foot square canvas. Her face was about twice life size. It was rare for me to look at one of my own paintings and like what I saw, but in this case I did. I carried it up and set it against the wall in Sara's living room. When she came out from the shower and saw it, she froze. There was a mix of shock and happiness in her face.

"It's my mother," she said. "I mean … it's her exactly. Did you paint this for my father?"

I hadn't expected Sara to confuse her own portrait with one of her mother, but I accepted the interpretation.

"Yes, I thought maybe he'd appreciate it."

"He'll love it," she said. "For as long as he can."

Chapter 39

THE VOICES ARE long gone, and now I have only myself to listen to. This time I can't blame the voices for leading me into the fire. This time I can't absolve myself of responsibility. It was my choice to put my son in danger. I should not have done that. This was one fire I should have ignored. Not for my own sake, but for William's. At least I was there to help him survive.

Still, the idea that I've been sabotaging him all this time, rather than aiding him, protecting him, is almost as unbearable as the idea of never seeing him again. I can't imagine how he must feel, wanting me gone while wanting me to never have left him in the first place. Part of me wants to be forgiven, but another part wants me to bear as much of this as possible so William might bear less of it. That, I now believe, can only be possible if I truly and finally depart.

The day I set myself on fire, though I failed at my primary objective, my death was in at least one sense a success. The voices in my head stopped and never returned. Still, I have yet to fulfill a promise I made to myself all those years ago: to leave this earth once and for all.

There isn't a primer on how to transition from one world to the next. No matter how many years I've been in this state of limbo, I can't say I've learned much about what I'm supposed to do next. But some things are clear. If I want to leave this world, I need to stop doing worldly things. I need to stop judging, stop grieving. No more intervening, no more painting.

And to finally and truly admit that my life is over, I need to return to the place where my death began.

There it sits, perfectly intact, our little suburban home, exactly as it was that day. Not a single sign of the fire. It's daytime, a beautiful day. I hear neighborhood kids playing, birds singing, and the breeze through the cottonwoods. That I'm finally hearing anything at all is miracle enough, but these are the most beautiful sounds—and among the only sounds—I have heard since the whoosh of the match strike all those years ago. These ordinary sounds are more visceral than I remember. The children's voices resonate in my chest. The chirps and warbles of the birds reverberate in my ears as if the creatures were perched on my shoulders. My hands, charred twigs for so long, have healed at last. And my brittle hair is soft again, free of dust and ash for the first time since the day it all went up in flames.

I pass into the house through the back door, the same way I escaped when it was burning to the ground. This time there is no smell of turpentine, no box of matches in my dress pocket. In the living room, my books are stacked in piles yet to be read. The old rocking chair is there, ready for another long night. I maneuver it back to William's room where I should have left it in the first place. I spot the telephone in the hallway. I dare not pick it up. The thought of a voice on the other end of the line still terrifies me, even now.

I descend the basement stairs. The old couch faces the stereo just as it always did. I sit down. The tubes of the amplifier glow a dim amber, and there is a record spinning. Behind me, my albums are neatly arranged on the shelves just as I had left them. Everything is perfect. But where is that can of turpentine? The matches? My pyramid? Nowhere to be seen. Neither are my paintings, easel, or brushes. Maybe I never needed any of those things.

Although a record is playing, no music emanates from the speakers. The needle dragging in the grooves makes the faintest sound, so it isn't my hearing. Maybe the stereo no longer cares to play music. I wonder which record it is. Joni? Joan? Aretha? Other than to go over and look, I have no way of knowing. But do I really want to know which record will be my last? Instead, I sit down on the couch and wait for the needle to start skipping at the end.

CHAPTER 40

ON THE NIGHT of Pigeonhole's concert, Sara and I walked downtown from her apartment rather than taking the train or an Uber. It was a beautiful night, and it had begun to snow lightly. I carried the cardboard Eddie Van Halen with me. We took our time crossing the Stone Arch Bridge, enjoying the views of the river as we walked. We arrived at First Avenue toward the end of the opening act, a Christian rock group called Burning Bush. I wasn't sorry to have missed them. Out on the sidewalk, the cardboard Eddie got a thumbs-up here and there from the vaping metal-heads, along with several cash offers, all of which I declined. I told them I needed to return him to his rightful owner. But I was worried that Eddie would be an issue at the door.

In the outer lobby, rows of tables held stacks of Bibles for sale alongside Pigeonhole T-shirts, bumper stickers, CDs, and crates of vinyl records. A security guard was particularly impressed by the cardboard Eddie, but said he would not be allowed in. I told him he belonged to Pigeonhole and that I had been his next-door neighbor.

He gasped. "You're ... the artist dude?"

I gasped back.

"All right, just this one time. I'm putting my job on the line here. Don't do anything dumb." He reached for his radio. "Attention all guards. Code metal—repeat—code metal. Cardboard Eddie coming through."

We walked onto the main floor. The crowd appeared to be mostly guitar dudes, but there were a few church basement dwellers, the odd corporate couple, and some random curiosities. Mainly, though, it was metal-heads—long hair, bad skin, tight pants, all standing shoulder to shoulder in solidarity. Their pious devotion to otherworldly guitar wizardry was palpable. I didn't know whether to laugh, cry, or drop dead.

"What, exactly, does this all mean?" I asked Sara.

"No idea," she said. "But I don't think I've ever seen so much hair product in one room. It's like we're at a concert in Fargo or something."

I nodded. "Fargo. Hair gel capital of the world."

The lights dimmed, and once again I heard that old, familiar hum. Many of the audience members made the sign of the cross against their chests. Even Sara did it. "Old habit," she said.

In true Pigeonhole fashion, he began playing offstage with a flurry of notes, which was immediately drowned out by screams of admiration. If air guitar could kill. A minute later, Pigeonhole rolled to center stage and a wall of amplifiers and speaker cabinets descended behind him as if from the heavens. Devotees conferred in each other's ears, likely about cabinet vintage, speaker cones, watts and ohms, new-old-stock vacuum tubes, and dual rectifiers. The furious crescendo of tapped notes went on so long, even I was impressed. The rest of the band joined in. But soon something happened, something I wasn't expecting.

Like a symphony conductor, Pigeonhole expertly brought the band to a halt with the wave of his hands. He signaled for silence from the audience. With both arms up, fingers spread, palms forward—a gesture more befitting a real wizard than a guitar wizard—he began to speak.

"Ladies and dudemen," he said, clearing his throat, "this is more than just a homecoming for me. It is a return to rock. Rock bottom, that is. Get it? Anyway, what I want you to hear, besides the metal you're about to receive, is this: If you're the kind of person who thinks there is no hope, then you don't even know what hope is. Hope isn't when there's still a chance. Hope is when you're out of chances. Hope is when you give up, completely. Hope is when you find God. May you find Him now."

With that, Pigeonhole launched into what I thought would be another laborious instrumental train wreck. But I was surprised to hear Van Halen's "Panama" with a female vocalist storming on stage with the flair of David Lee Roth. After a minute I realized it was Tanya. She had gained some much-needed weight, and her acrobatics showed she had clearly been working out. The song was short and sweet, and I breathed a sigh of relief.

The concert was nearly ninety minutes long and consisted of twenty-odd songs, most of them covers from the guitar rock pantheon: "Crossroads," "Gimmie All Your Lovin'," "Crazy Train," "Highway to Hell" (the only song the guitar dudes danced to, for whatever reason), "Money for Nothing," "Hallowed Be Thy Name," "Enter Sandman," "Voodoo Chile," "Stairway to Heaven," and even an extended-solo version of "Purple Rain," on which Tanya sang beautifully. After the first encore—a death metal rendition of "Smoke on the Water"—I picked up the cardboard Eddie.

"This is it," I said to Sara. "I'm going in."

I approached the stage. A security guard touched the earpiece in her ear and reached for her radio. Then she recognized Eddie's disarming smile and gave me a polite nod. I stood beneath the stage and turned around to face the audience. I was bathed in white light—clean, heavenly, rockstar light—so much purer than firelight.

I raised Eddie up over my head. As hard as I could, I hurtled him onto the stage. I had attached a weight to the foot of the cutout in hopes of it landing upright. To my relief, it landed just a few feet in front of Pigeonhole and teetered to a standstill. Pigeonhole stopped playing. He took off his guitar and let it fall to the floor, just as he had that fateful night. The entire room went silent. Pigeonhole started to sob as he rolled over to Eddie and embraced him. "Eddie, forgive me!" he bellowed several times in a row, his headset microphone picking up every word.

Pigeonhole's bass player walked over and picked up his guitar, handing it back to him like a mortal returning Thor's hammer. Pigeonhole let go of Eddie and broke into a note-for-note, pitch-perfect rendition of Van Halen's "Eruption." The crowd roared with a deafening fervor. The next song was, naturally, "You Really Got Me," and finally, fittingly, "Runnin' with the Devil."

As the final song concluded, someone came up behind me and tapped me on the shoulder. I was terrified that it was my mother. When I turned around, I was relieved and grateful to see it was Sara. The look on her face reminded me of the first time I saw her at that outdoor concert: beautiful, hopeful, still a little reckless. She pointed to the balcony. Clarissa and Einstein were in attendance. I might have known. Clarissa waved, tepidly, as if she were an obscure royal. Instinctively I scanned the ceiling, half expecting my mother to be hanging from a set of stage lights. But—deep down—I knew I would never see my mother again in this world.

ACKNOWLEDGMENTS

So MANY PEOPLE played a role in making this book possible. In no particular order, I would like to offer my heartfelt gratitude to the following people, institutions, and communities.

To StoryStudio and its faculty, especially Abby Geni and Rebecca Makkai. To Elizabeth Gaffney at A Public Space. To the Loft Literary Center, the Minnesota State Arts Board, and the Minneapolis Institute of Art. To Kansas State University for naming this book a finalist for the 2024 American Buffalo Books Fiction Prize. To Bill Burleson at Flexible Press for publishing it. And to every early reader, especially my fellow students at StoryStudio and A Public Space.

To the many writers and editors who (knowingly or unknowingly) dropped the breadcrumbs that led me through deep, dark woods of completing my first novel: Sheila O'Connor, Christopher Castellani, Mary Rockcastle, David Treuer, Peter Geye, Brianna Low, Toni Halleen, Rebecca Kanner, Ethan Rutherford, Brad Zellar, Benjamin Percy, Jeanne Platt, Josie Sigler Sibara, Stephanie Wilbur Ash, Sarah Stonich, John Jodzio, Julie Schumacher, Lara Avery, Ben Barnhart, Dylan Hicks, Matt Rasmussen, David Schwartz, Robert Voedisch, Daniel Hornsby, Sequoia Nagamatsu, Curtis Sittenfeld, Sally Franson, Donald Ray Pollock,

Dan Chaon, Matt Bell, Kevin Maloney, Lauren Groff, Steve Almond, Maurice Carlos Ruffin, Robert Olen Butler, George Saunders, Lorrie Moore, Scott McClanahan, Gabe Habash, Andy Mozina, Tom Drury, and so many more.

To librarians and booksellers everywhere. All of you should be rich and famous.

To guitarists and the guitar community, for teaching me joy intertwined with awe. To name but a few: Eddie Van Halen, Wolfgang Van Halen, Prince, Shuggie Otis, Steve Lukather, Joe Walsh, June Millington, Jesse Johnson, Marty Stuart, Yngwie Malmsteen, Waddy Wachtel, Molly Tuttle, Peter Frampton, Chuck Berry, John Scofield, Ed King, Carol Kaye, Guthrie Govan, Dweezil Zappa, Jennifer Batten, Pat Metheny, Steve Vai, Wendy Malvoin, Dez Dickerson, Kevin Schafer, David Hanbury (Mrs. Smith), Andrew French, Slim Dunlap, Jack White, Carlos Santana, Buddy Guy, Billy Strings, Brian Setzer, Billy Gibbons, Rick Beato (who is tired of your excuses!), and countless others. And to every garage and basement player, a shocking number of whom are truly great, as social media has revealed. Keep on rocking.

And finally to my mother, Elizabeth, for her loving, endless acts of irreverent vision, and to the voices, whose echoes remain.

ABOUT THE AUTHOR

STEVEN LAWRENCE LANG is a writer, an artist, an orphan, a father, and a frustrated guitar player from St. Paul, Minnesota. His fiction has appeared in various print and online publications including *CutBank*, *Chestnut Review*, *Slush Pile Magazine*, *Catamaran*, *Prime Number Magazine*, *Stonecoast Review*, *Fiction on a Stick* (Milkweed Editions), and *The Art of Wonder* (University of Minnesota Press). He uses a capo and knows all three chords.

Visit www.stevenlang.net for more information.

"*The Art of Falling Apart* has something for everyone: toxic love, a haunting, an unfinished portrait, a thirst for vengeance, an exploration of the power of art in all its forms, and a life-sized cardboard cutout of Eddie Van Halen. If you want to snort-laugh, gasp, marvel, relate, tear up, and keep turning pages, this is the book for you. It is a quirky, unputdownable delight."—Abby Geni, author of *The Lightkeepers*

"Haunting and haunted, Steven Lang's *The Art of Falling Apart* is a seriocomic novel whose alternating narrators differ not only in their points of view but in their planes of existence. Set with a careful eye in the Twin Cities, it's a darkly comic, soulful, and musical exploration of essential themes: heredity, grief, art, inspiration, talent, class, love."—Dylan Hicks, author of *Boarded Windows* and *Amateurs*

"Inventive, offbeat, and unexpectedly moving, The Art of Falling Apart follows a struggling painter whose greatest work may not be entirely his own—and whose complicated bond with his dead mother refuses to stay buried. With humor and emotional bite, it charts romantic misfires, artistic doubt, and the eerie intimacy of grief. Strange and tender in equal measure, it's a story about creativity, love, and becoming your own person."—Rebecca Kanner, author of *Last One Seen*

"The Art of Falling Apart is a darkly funny and deeply true exploration of human flaws and our shared yearning for connection, rendered bingeable through its perfect prose. Juxtaposing grief and imagination, Lang paints vivid interior worlds, highlighting what we see and don't see, and calling our hearts to settle on what really matters. I loved it."—Toni Halleen, author of *The Surrogate* and *The Good Samaritan*

The Art of
Falling Apart

Steven Lawrence Lang

Flexible Press

Minneapolis, Minnesota, 2026

COPYRIGHT © 2026 Steven Lawrence Lang
All Rights Reserved. This is a work of fiction.
Names, characters, places, and incidents are the products of
the author's imagination, and any resemblance to an actual
person, living or dead, events, or locales is
entirely coincidental.

Print ISBN: 979-8-9998771-7-8
eBook ISBN: 979-8-9998771-8-5

Flexible Press LLC
Minneapolis, Minnesota
www.flexiblepub.com
Editors William E Burleson,
Vicki Adang, Mark My Words Editorial Services, LLC
Cover by Steven Lawrence Lang, photo by Anthony Day

www.ingramcontent.com/pod-product-compliance
Lightning Source LLC
Chambersburg PA
CBHW020335180726

47991CB00020B/1711